LOVE ME

DELANEY DIAMOND

GARDEN AVENUE PRESS

Love Me by Delaney Diamond

Copyright © 2020, Delaney Diamond

Garden Avenue Press

Atlanta, Georgia

ISBN: 978-1-946302-27-4 (Ebook edition)

ISBN: 978-1-946302-28-1 (Paperback edition)

www.delaneydiamond.com

PROLOGUE

Axel reclined against the pillows in the hotel bed, the rumpled sheets covering his nakedness as he watched her pull the dress over her head. The light, floral fabric slid lower and covered her bow-shaped hips before falling in a whisper to her knees.

As she leaned into the mirror to apply lipstick, tightness squeezed his chest muscles. His time with her had been nothing short of phenomenal, but she was about to walk out of his life, and he'd never see her again because they'd withheld vital details from each other. He didn't even know her name. At least, he didn't think he did. The name she'd given was almost certainly fake. *Andrea,* she'd answered when he asked—clumsily, awkwardly—but it didn't fit. She didn't *look* like an Andrea.

Axel threw back the covers. The two-week vacation in Belize had been a sort of congratulatory gift to himself for winning a case that had dogged the firm for three years and established him as a force to be reckoned with in corporate law. The resort and beach were mostly empty, since coming here in October meant a much more quiet, relaxing vacation than he would have had during the high season. Meeting her five days into said vacation had been an unexpected bonus, and for five days and four nights he'd thought of little else but putting a smile on her face and losing himself in her delectable body.

Completely nude, Axel strolled to where she stood examining her features as she fiddled with her curly raven hair, trying to figure out the perfect style. He stopped directly behind her and captured the pleasing floral scent of the coconut-hibiscus cream she rubbed all over her body.

Their eyes met in the mirror. Hers were dark, with long, thick lashes that conveyed a come-hither look without trying. She arched a groomed eyebrow.

"You look fine," he said, placing a hand on either side of her on the dresser. He whispered the next words in her ear while maintaining eye contact. "You look stunning. If you didn't have to leave, I'd take you back to bed."

She laughed—sultry, confident. Way more confident than when he'd approached her at the pool. Initially, she'd been... shy? No, hesitant. Her eyes had even held a bit of sadness.

The lime-green bikini against her dusky-dark skin had caught his eye, and by cursory observation, also caught the eye of the other two men poolside. He'd been the lucky bastard there alone and took the initiative to approach her.

"You're quite the flatterer, you know that? I'm going back home with an inflated ego."

"And where is home?"

Their eyes locked. "You know I can't tell you that," she said quietly.

"You won't tell me," he corrected.

"Same difference." She shrugged.

"Persistence is key in my line of work."

"Good for you. I'm sure you're great at whatever you do."

"I'm great at a lot of things. I'd like to tell you more about me."

"But I'd rather not know." Her voice took on an edge.

Frustration ate at him. This situation was ridiculous. He was used to working hard, and hard work resulted in a reward of some kind, yet no matter how much he pushed, she wouldn't budge an inch on them sharing more information with each other.

"So, you're just going to leave?" He straightened.

She turned to face him and tipped back her head. "I thought we understood each other, Axel."

He'd given her his real name and was glad he did. The sound of her panting those four letters during each orgasm was branded into his brain.

"Do we? I understand that you're about to leave without giving me any more information about yourself, though we both had a great time on this trip."

"And that's all it was—a great time. Today I go back to reality." She dropped her gaze and eased past him.

He caught her arm above the elbow and forced her gaze higher. There was something in her voice. Regret. Disappointment. She didn't want to go back to the life she left, wherever that was.

"Stay another day with me."

"I can't." She shook her head slowly, regretfully. "I *can't* give you anything more. If we're meant to be, we'll meet again."

The tightness in his chest increased. She was really going to leave, and he'd have nothing but memories and a fake name.

"You can give me something else. One more time," Axel said. His need for her overwhelmed him, and that need was obvious in the heated sound of his voice.

He may not know much about her, but he knew that her need matched his, and if he touched her just right, her body would go up in flames like it did every time since they first made love.

Axel bent his head and tasted her lips. They were wide and

full and downright delicious. "One more time," he whispered against her mouth.

Her right hand caressed his chest, gliding over the tight nipples on his pecs before smoothing over the hair-roughened skin of his abs. His body hardened, and she paused at his left hip, her gaze focused on his rigid flesh.

"One more time," she said shakily.

Then she licked her lips, and that did it. Axel crushed her mouth beneath his and lifted her from the carpet. Her soft moans filled his ears as he carried her to the bed. He placed her across the mattress and swiftly dragged her panties past her ankles and tossed them to the floor. He dropped several kisses at the apex of her thighs, inhaling her feminine scent and savoring his last taste of heaven.

He hurriedly put on a condom, and with desperation born from gut-rending hunger, he sliced his length into her and began to thrust in earnest. His hips drove hard between her thighs. Bending his head, he showered her throat and face with kisses. How was he supposed to forget her after this? How the hell could he go back to the emptiness his life used to be?

Her fingernails clawed his back and ass, and he flinched against the pain that simultaneously brought pleasure. With a rough groan, he continued to drive into her. Their shallow breaths beat against each other, eyes wide open and gazes bound together as if by a rope of yearning and a plea for more.

As she came, her eyes shuttered closed and her head fell back. Her lips parted on a sound that sent shivers down his spine as she cried out his name one last time—her voice bouncing back and forth against the walls.

~

THE BOARDING ANNOUNCEMENT had come several minutes ago. Soon they'd call her zone, and she'd be on her way back to

Atlanta. Back to an existence that seemed like a death sentence after her time with him.

Find me, and maybe there'll be another chance for us. That's what she'd told him, knowing good and well she'd given him a fake name and zero information. He'd never be able to find her.

Axel. Is that his real name? Naphressa wondered.

Didn't matter. She'd never forget him or the way he made her feel. She hadn't been whole in so long, but this short trip and the time she spent with him had changed her perspective on her lot in life.

She felt alive. Renewed. More like her old self.

She tapped out the obligatory text. *Boarding soon.*

Seconds later, the response came from her sister. *Enjoyed your trip?*

Just what I needed.

Good. See you soon. Love you.

See you soon. Love you too.

"Zone four. We are now boarding zone four," the airline attendant said over the speaker.

Naphressa stood with her carry-on and joined the line of passengers. After getting settled in her seat by the window, she slid open the zipper of the pocket inside her purse and slipped out the gold band. She needed to do this before she forgot.

She placed the ring on the wedding finger of her left hand and, closing her eyes, rested her head against the seat.

Back to reality.

1

Axel strolled into Double Trouble Bar, and immediately the tension from the week lifted off his shoulders. Today in particular had been long and tense, with a potential conflict headed to court, but at the last minute he'd managed to negotiate a truce between his side and the opposing counsel. As a corporate attorney at the law firm of Abraham, MacKenzie & Wong, there was never a dull moment, and today, he'd earned the drinks he was about to have.

"Heyyy, Axel," a waitress crooned, flashing him a flirtatious smile as she passed by with a tray full of drinks.

"Hey, Lisa," he returned, biting his bottom lip. He paused a few seconds, casting a glance over his shoulder to appreciate her shapely figure as she walked away.

She'd made no secret of her interest, and though he found her attractive, he decided against hooking up since he visited the bar at least once a week. Coming here would become awkward when they didn't work out.

He spotted his two buddies at the end of the bar and headed that way. For three years, almost from the day they met during a basketball league, the three men had been coming here on a weekly basis to unwind and catch up.

"Look who finally made it," Cole remarked.

Colton "Cole" Eubanks was tall, with golden brown skin and a full beard. An investment manager, he co-owned the bar with his sister, Dani.

"Don't start, I had a rough day. What's the score?" Axel glanced at the basketball game playing on one of the televisions behind the bar. Having left his tie and jacket in the car, he rolled up the sleeves of his light blue shirt.

"Seventy-nine, seventy-seven. Hawks have the lead," Cole answered.

Axel sat next to Braxton Harper, a computer network architect with walnut-brown skin and a close beard. He was the third member of the trio. Axel waved at Dani behind the bar, and she nodded to let him know she'd seen him and would soon come over with his rum and Coke.

"What were you working on that had you running late?" Braxton asked, before taking a long drag on his beer.

"A licensing agreement almost fell apart." He launched into a general explanation without giving details that would breach the confidentiality of his clients.

During the talk, Dani dropped off his drink and he ordered some wings. In the meantime, he noshed on pretzels from the wooden bowl on the bar top.

"Do you ever get tired of these close calls?" Braxton asked.

"You'd think I would, but I love it. Gets my blood pumping."

"There are better ways to get the blood pumping," Dani said, setting the basket of wings in front of him. She placed a hand on one hip and challenged him with her eyes.

"I'm going to assume you're talking about women, and I agree. Except sometimes I wonder if your gender is worth the trouble. Finding a good one is like finding a needle in a haystack, and you're unpredictable. Frankly, right now I'd rather have a root canal than deal with women and your random mood swings."

Cole and Braxton chuckled.

Ignoring them, Dani asked, "Didn't you almost get married once?"

"Almost."

"And...?"

"And what? It didn't work out." He shrugged one shoulder.

"Your fault or hers?"

"What do you think?" Axel spread his arms as if to say, *Look at me, I'm the total package.*

Dani rolled her eyes.

"Ignore my sister. As usual, she thinks she knows everything and is dipping into grown men's business." Cole held up his empty glass. "Another Scotch, please."

"I'm grown, too, and I happen to know a thing or two about women. More than the three of you put together." Dani pointed at each of them individually.

"Thanks, Dani. You're always such a breath of fresh air during our conversations," Axel said.

She narrowed her eyes and he winked at her, forcing a reluctant smile from her lips. "Whatever, Axel. Another Scotch, coming up," she said to her brother.

As often happened, the conversation shifted to women and the three of them started complaining about the difficulty they'd had in finding good women to marry. Valentine's Day had taken place a week ago, and Axel hadn't sent flowers to anyone but his mother and a great aunt in Michigan. His assistant knew to purchase herself a meal and her favorite chocolates. That had been the extent of his Valentine's Day gift-giving, but he missed making a woman he cared about smile by buying her gifts or taking her on a trip somewhere.

"Women don't know what they want, anyway," Braxton

grumbled. "They say they want one thing, but they always go for the opposite."

"No point in trying to figure them out," Cole said.

"I hear you," Axel agreed.

Dani was once again in front of them, this time with both hands on her hips. "I'm so tired of hearing the three of you complain. You guys are idiots. Let me tell you what your problems are. Axel, you're too withdrawn and emotionally unavailable to women. Though you make jokes, it's probably because of how your engagement ended. Braxton, you're waiting for a *perfect* woman. She doesn't exist because no one is perfect. If you stopped being so picky, you might find someone. And you, my dear brother, are the most self-centered man to walk the face of the earth. You guys are never getting married until you make some changes."

"Hold up," Axel said, straightening on the stool.

"What makes you the authority on why we aren't married and won't, according to you, ever get married?" Cole asked.

"The three of you come in here at least once a week griping about this woman or that woman. I listen, and it's the same complaints every time. You think someone is always after your money or trying to use you in some way," she said to Cole. "And Axel, the way you go through women, how is it possible you haven't found anyone yet? Could it be because you refuse to open up?"

"That's a bit harsh. I date a lot, but I wouldn't say I go *through* women," Axel muttered.

"So you say." She arched an eyebrow and then walked off.

After Dani's verbal takedown, they all fell silent.

Axel frowned into his rum and Coke. What Dani had said wasn't news. He'd heard those comments about himself from his own mother. He'd even heard the words *cool* and *aloof* thrown out by a woman or two.

He wanted to get married, but he'd been burned before. He

and his ex-fiancée, Rose, had talked in detail about the life they planned to live together—the number of kids they wanted and where they wanted them to go to school, annual vacations, and which part of town they wanted to live in. She'd been enamored with Brookhaven, a northeastern suburb of Atlanta filled with historic homes, which in recent years had seen an increase in commercial developments. He'd purchased a home for them in that area—a four-bedroom with four bathrooms, a basement, and a spacious yard in a community of equally large homes.

Yet as the time drew nearer for their wedding, they encountered an insurmountable obstacle. As a pharmaceutical rep, Rose was offered a promotion to be sales manager over her own team, but the promotion meant moving to Maryland. In the end, their arguments and heated conversations resulted in a conclusion he'd seen coming from afar. He did his best to push back on her decision, but in the end, she took the job, and their relationship fell apart. She couldn't pass up this opportunity, and he didn't want to leave his work and being near his parents in Augusta.

So was it any surprise that he was a bit...cautious when it came to relationships?

The three of them continued talking, but the tone of their conversation had changed. Dani had gotten inside their heads —at least, inside his, and her comments made him think about the one woman he hadn't been able to forget since he met her. The one woman whose beauty and personality eclipsed everyone else. With whom he hadn't been withdrawn or aloof. Andrea, the woman he met in Belize sixteen months ago.

Where was she now? The desire to see her again hadn't extinguished, and Dani's words made them flare to life again. Maybe he should take another trip to Belize and see if he could dig up some information on her, because despite his reluctance to agree with Dani, her suggestion had been right. He had become emotionally unavailable to other women since his engagement ended.

But with Andrea, he'd been wide open. He let his guard down and enjoyed himself immensely. She made him laugh, their teasing and playfulness completely natural though they'd only known each other a short time. He wanted that feeling again.

Once, in his twenties, he'd looked at his parents joking around in the kitchen and wondered what it would be like to find someone he connected with on the same level. Someone who not only made him laugh, but someone he could sit quietly in a room with—not saying a word to each other for an hour stretch at a time—and still be content.

Later that evening, after his mother had retired to bed and he and his father were smoking Cubans on the back porch, he watched the smoke curl upward into the night and asked his father the same question men had been asking their fathers for centuries.

"How did you know Mom was the one?"

His father idly examined his cigar and puffed smoke through his lips. Finally, he looked at Axel with a smile and said, *"When you find her, you'll know. Trust me. And no one else will do."*

He hadn't fully understood the answer and had been mildly annoyed because he'd wanted concrete advice. Something tangible he could lock away and pull out to examine as the need arose.

Then he went to Belize, and his father's words finally made sense.

No doubt about it. He had to find Andrea. Because no one else would do.

2

After two brief knocks, Naphressa's door popped open. Standing at her bookcase with building plans in hand, she watched as Loretta, the administrative assistant she shared with two other project managers, waltzed in with papers and Naphressa's breakfast.

"One coffee. One toasted everything-bagel with extra cream cheese. Two sets of contracts." The buxom redhead underlined the words by plopping the items one by one on her over-crowded desk.

With a grateful moan, Naphressa abandoned the project plans she'd been studying and rushed over to the desk. "I'm starving. Thank you, you're a godsend."

She opened the paper sack, sniffed the contents, and sighed with happiness as the scent of bread and coffee filled her nostrils.

Loretta placed a hand on one expansive hip. "Skinny as you are, darlin', you need more than a bagel and coffee. You need some protein, too, like eggs and bacon for sustenance and to put some meat on your bones."

Naphressa hid a smile as she sank onto her leather chair

and started removing the items from the bag. She'd gotten used to Loretta's mothering since she started working in project management for Hayes Realty Management a few years ago. Loretta was always performing some selfless task for a member of the staff. This week alone, she'd seen her organize a surprise birthday party, bake a five-year work anniversary cake for one of the appraisers, collect clothes for an auditor who lost his house in a fire, and bring in a large container of homemade chicken soup for a property manager whose wife was sick with a cold.

It's not as if she didn't have a family of her own. Her husband had recently retired and was "underfoot," as she called it, and on the weekends she took care of her widower son's three kids so he could work a part-time job. Overall, Loretta was the kind of woman who had your back, and if she seemed a bit pushy because of it—well, you just had to deal.

"I've told you before, I have a high metabolism," Naphressa said.

"I don't know nothing 'bout that. Been a big girl all my life. Never lost my baby fat." Loretta slapped her hip.

"I bet Earl doesn't mind," Naphressa said with a smile.

"Oh, honey, he sure don't. From day one he told me, 'I love you the way you are,' and that ain't never changed. After thirty-one years, he still says the same thing. Reckon I'll keep him." Loretta laughed and headed toward the door. She paused on her way out. "I'm gonna need those contracts signed before you leave for the day."

"I'll have them to you in an hour."

After Loretta left, Naphressa smothered cream cheese onto her bagel. She took a bite, eyes going to the pictures of her nephews and niece on the desk. Her sister and her husband had four kids, but the picture that drew her eyes was the one of Regina, the ten-month-old. After three boys, they'd been desperate for a little girl and finally got her.

In the photo, she was only two months out of the hospital and looked adorable lying on her back in a yellow onesie with green turtles all over it. The photographer had captured her joy, her eyes shiny, mouth wide with laughter.

Naphressa picked up the photo and examined her niece's features. She adored this little girl. She might be the closest she ever came to having a daughter of her own for a while.

She gave her head a brisk shake, refusing to give in to the longing today. She intended to stay happy. She'd orchestrated the biggest project of her career only weeks before and was grateful. She would celebrate the little victories.

Naphressa sipped her coffee and picked up the stack of contracts to start her review so she could have them signed and back to Loretta within the timeframe she promised.

AXEL PACKED UP HIS DESK, ready for lunch. Grabbing his jacket, he exited the door and almost ran into one of the younger attorneys, Anton.

"Whoa," he said, taking a step back.

Anton had a fork and a plate of cake in his hands. "You're leaving?" he asked.

"Hell yeah, I'm leaving. It's past lunchtime and I'm starving." Axel started down the hall and Anton fell into step beside him.

"Got a question for you."

"Shoot," Axel said, not breaking stride.

"I have an issue with a new client. I—"

"Where'd you get that from?" Axel asked, nodding toward the cake.

Anton looked at the dessert as if he suddenly realized it was in his hands. "This? At the welcome-to-the-office luncheon for the new associates."

"That was today?"

He hardly paid attention to emails for those types of office events. The only ones he paid attention to were the compulsory ones. Since attendance had been voluntary, he'd deleted the invite as soon as it arrived in his box, not bothering to read the details because he had no intention of going. In a firm with hundreds of attorneys, he was certain he hadn't been missed.

His mind flashed back to the adjectives Dani used to describe him Friday night. *Withdrawn. Emotionally unavailable.* He grimaced.

"Yes, that was today," Anton replied.

"Any cake left?"

Anton shook his head as he chewed. "I had this hidden away in my office. So, about that question..."

Tall, with brown skin and light eyes, he was thirty, seven years younger than Axel, but had only been with the firm for a few years. He also worked in corporate law. In a lot of ways, he reminded Axel of himself when he first started practicing— focused, driven. He expected Anton to go far and had taken him under his wing to offer advice whenever he could.

"Go ahead, but you'll have to follow me." Axel hit the *down* button on the elevator.

Anton explained about the problems his client was having renegotiating employee benefits and salary ever since they decided to restructure the company because it had been losing money for years. The owners couldn't agree on what to offer the employees.

Axel listened, interjecting an occasional question, and at the end told Anton, "Some of the employees might be ready to walk, and that's something they should find out sooner rather than later. If so, they could work out a severance package and then negotiate with the ones who remain. Talk to Stevens over in employment law. He had a similar problem about a year ago and could help with some of those details."

Anton nodded. "Makes sense. Thanks, man."

"How are things going with that Hayes Realty deal?" Axel asked.

"So far so good."

The elevator doors opened. Jason Thurman, one of the partners, said, "Axel, just the man I wanted to see. Anton, I need to talk to you, too. Got a minute?" Jason stepped out of the cabin.

Axel groaned inwardly. He needed food. No telling how long this impromptu meeting would last, but when a partner wanted to meet with you, you couldn't exactly say no.

"Sure, I've got a few minutes," he replied.

"Excellent. We've run into a bit of a problem on the Hayes Realty deal. Originally, I had Simons overseeing the case, but I had to pull her onto another case. Axel, I want you to take over."

"Simons is off completely?" Anton asked, sounding worried.

Jason nodded. "Axel, you can get up to speed, can't you? Anton, give him a quick rundown of what's going on."

"We're meeting with the team from Hayes Realty in..." Anton glanced at his watch. "Less than an hour."

"All the more reason to get started right away, wouldn't you say?" Jason shot them a smile that indicated he knew they'd do exactly that.

"Not a problem," Axel said.

"Good, good." Jason went down the hall.

"Shit," Anton muttered.

"Should I be offended that you don't want me on this case?" Axel asked.

"It's not that I don't want you, it's that now you have to catch up. It's early yet, but we've done a lot of groundwork and we're ready to go."

"I have every confidence in you. Tell you what, put together a summary page for me. Bullet points for now to get me through the meeting. I'll be back from lunch in about thirty and that'll give me enough time to review the details and ask questions, if I have any. I'll do a more thorough review later."

"Sounds like a plan. We're meeting in conference room B on the fourth floor at two."

"I'll be there."

Anton went left down the hallway, and Axel took the elevator to the first floor. He escaped into the parking lot with a few head nods to other staff and the security guards at the front.

Since he couldn't take a leisurely lunch elsewhere as planned, he settled for a sandwich and drink at the café across the street. By the time he returned to the office, Anton had sent the bullet-point summary with the names of the project manager and other contacts at Hayes Realty Management.

The real estate firm specialized in commercial real estate, and though Axel didn't know much about them, he knew enough to know they had built a solid reputation in Atlanta. The current deal saw them in a unique position. After finding out that The Brixton Group was going bankrupt because they'd overextended themselves on a real estate development project, Hayes Realty had swooped in and made an offer to take over the cash-strapped company and all their assets for ridiculously low prices.

The deal was currently hush-hush so that The Brixton Group could save face. The purchase would be spun as a merger, and the dozens of employees who would have lost their jobs if the company was dissolved, could keep their jobs or find new positions within Hayes Realty.

They intended to hire Abraham, MacKenzie & Wong to aid in working out the details. Axel only had a few questions and was ready for the meeting by the time two o'clock rolled around.

As he opened the conference room door, Axel's eyes swept

the interior. Anton and the other attorney on the case—a tall blonde named Jen, were already inside. His eyes landed on the third person in the room, and he froze.

Everything froze. Time. His body. His breathing. His heart.

He blinked, but what he thought was a mirage was very real. It was *her*. Andrea, in the flesh.

All he could see was the back of her head as she chatted with his co-workers, but there was no doubt in his mind that the person he saw was Andrea, the woman he met in Belize.

Heart racing, he set his pen and notepad on the table. Eyes pinned in disbelief on the figure before him, he ate up the distance between them.

Anton saw him first. "Hi, Axel."

Andrea then faced him, and his mouth went dry. Same dusky-dark skin and raven hair that spiraled to her shoulders in wide, lustrous curls that framed her face. Her black skirt and black jacket came in at the waist and showed off slim curves that he'd traced with his tongue and fingertips over and over again.

"It *is* you," he whispered.

Her pretty eyes widened.

"Andrea, what are you doing here?" Axel asked.

Anton and the other attorney frowned.

"Andrea? No, this is Naphressa St. James, the project manager from Hayes Realty Management," Anton said.

"You're with Hayes," Axel murmured, barely registering what his co-worker said.

He was on autopilot, entranced by the woman who'd haunted his nights for over a year. No one had compared to her before or since.

"How have you been?" he asked.

"I..." She shifted from one foot to the next and darted a quick glance at Anton and Jen.

Anton nudged the blonde. "We have to get some paperwork that I forgot to bring in. Be back in a few minutes."

The two of them disappeared, but Axel barely noticed. He hadn't lifted his gaze from *Naphressa*. The name fit much better than Andrea.

"Damn, I can't believe it's you."

"It's me," she said, looking twitchy, as if she were nervous.

"This is a shock."

"For me, too."

He lowered his voice. "This isn't the time or place, but maybe you and I could—"

She shook her head. "No."

"You haven't heard what I was about to say."

Her eyes pleaded with him for understanding. "I don't have to hear what you're about to say. I know what you're going to say. It's about the challenge that I made to you before we left Belize."

"You told me to find you, and I've been looking."

"I should have never told you to do that."

"You said there would be a chance for us."

"*Maybe*," she corrected.

"Okay, look, I know this is all very sudden and my firm is working on a case for you, and I understand the ethical implications, but we met before this deal. If you prefer, I could ask to be taken off the project."

"You do whatever you feel is best. I, however, have no intention of getting involved with you. I said *maybe* there was a chance for us, and I shouldn't have said that. Shouldn't have implied there was a possibility we could get together if we met again."

Axel gave a shallow, pain-filled laugh. "My ego is taking quite a bruising right now. Care to explain why there's no possibility of us getting together again?"

"I... It's..." She licked her lips, clearly unable to come up with a reasonable explanation.

"Look—" Axel stopped abruptly and stared at the gold ring on her finger as shock reverberated through his chest. "Are you *married?*"

3

Outwardly calm, Naphressa quaked inside from shock.

Axel looked every bit as handsome as he did in Belize. Only now, he was polished, too, in a navy suit and navy and burgundy tie. Suave and smooth with a low-cut beard and sharp, assessing eyes, he made her want to squirm to hide her immediate elation at seeing him again.

"I'm no longer married."

"But you're wearing a wedding ring."

Sometimes she forgot she still wore her wedding ring. It was just a piece of jewelry now, like the gold bracelet on her wrist and the matching necklace around her neck. She took it off every night along with the other pieces, hating that she had to wear it all. It was like a chain, binding her to a dead man.

Nodding, she twisted the ring on her finger. "It's complicated. My husband is...dead. I was married to Victor Hayes' son —Byron Hayes. He was a good man, a hero." She was embarrassed by how stilted and stale the words sounded, as if they'd been rehearsed and repeated numerous times. Which they had been. She needed to do better. Sound more convincing.

"I'm sorry."

Axel's voice reminded her that she wasn't alone and forced her focus on the conversation, which meant she paid closer attention to him. That was a mistake. She'd thought about him often, and seeing him again made her heart and body ache.

Axel had a solid, athletic build. His tailored suit fit snug over his body, showing off broad shoulders, lean hips, and long legs. From the top of his head to his feet, he looked well put together. His black, curly hair was neatly trimmed, his beard and mustache cut low and framing lips that had wreaked havoc on her body, making her loathe leaving his bed to eat or even sightsee. She would have been quite content to spend the entire trip wrapped in his arms.

Then, of course, there was his obsession. His fixation. He liked going down on her. Not every man enjoyed doing that to a woman, but Axel—*good heavens*—he clearly did. Almost every time they made love, he rewarded her with his head between her legs. If practice made perfect, he'd certainly perfected his technique. The man was an absolute beast with his tongue—an aficionado, one who could teach a master class in the art of cunnilingus.

"Life isn't perfect." She took a deep breath. "You work here?"

"I'm a senior associate in corporate law," Axel answered. "What do you do for Hayes Realty?"

"My official title is project manager," Naphressa answered. "But I represent the company in all major real estate projects, acting as a go-between in pretty much anything involving the company—from purchasing property to purchasing businesses."

"How long have you been doing that?"

"A few years. I started in property management and worked my way up." She tilted her chin a little higher, proud of her accomplishments. Not bad for a girl with no college education.

"So you've been in Atlanta for a while."

"I was born here."

Axel huffed out a breath. "I can't believe this. All this time you've been right here, and now I've accidentally run into you when I doubted I'd ever see you again." He looked stunned.

"Small world," Naphressa said quietly.

She didn't know how to say everything she needed to say. She wanted to tell him how difficult it had been to leave him that day, especially after their last intense bout of lovemaking. She wanted to explain the sense of loss she'd experienced on the flight back to Atlanta—how she'd almost run into the cockpit and begged the pilot to turn the plane around. She'd never forgotten him or the way he'd made her feel—alive for the first time in a long time. Treasured. Special.

"Axel, I—"

"You know—"

They spoke at the same time and stopped at the same time.

"You go first," he said.

"No, you," Naphressa insisted, glad for the extra time.

He opened his mouth and then stopped. He clearly didn't know what to say, either.

"I never forgot our time in Belize. I did search for you." The words came out gravelly, as if they scraped his throat on the way up.

"It was a brief moment in time when I needed to let go, and you gave me that opportunity."

"It doesn't have to be the last time you let go," Axel whispered, eyes intense.

Her knees weakened at the need in his voice.

She swallowed as disappointment tightened her heart. "I don't think it would be a good idea for me to screw the attorney at the firm working with my company—a company owned by my dead husband's parents. Quite a dilemma."

"A dilemma that could be overcome. Naphressa, I still want

you. I can't pretend like Belize never happened. How am I supposed to forget that? We had a connection."

"We had sex," she countered, pretending their time together meant significantly less to her than it really did.

His eyes flashed angrily. "It was more than sex, and you know it."

"Nothing can happen between us, Axel."

"What do you mean, nothing—"

"Look who we found," Anton said, coming into the room.

Following behind him was the blonde attorney, Jen, and Ezekiel, a Hayes Realty property manager whom everyone referred to as Zeke. The fourth person was one of the real estate firm's in-house attorneys. They were followed closely by a young woman pushing a rolling tray with coffee, tea, and a choice of pastries.

"I guess we can get started now," Naphressa said, easing away from Axel, able to breathe normally again.

She took a seat on the opposite side of the table from the two attorneys from Axel's firm, watching surreptitiously as Axel walked over to the refreshments cart.

He made himself a coffee, sipping while they reviewed the paperwork and discussed how to proceed with the negotiations between Hayes Realty Management and The Brixton Group. Her mind wandered a bit but came back to the room when she heard laughter. The conversation had shifted.

"I'm not the best at it," Zeke was saying, running fingers through his brown hair. "I like to paint, but it's more like paint by numbers. One of these days I'm going to take a class so I can get really good. Naphressa's actually a great artist."

All eyes turned to her.

"I'm not *great*," she demurred.

"Don't be modest. She does watercolors, and they're really good. She has a bunch of them hanging in her office at work."

"Everyone needs a hobby, something to help you relax outside of work," Jen interjected.

"What's yours?" Zeke asked, his eyes displaying more than a passing interest in her extracurricular activities.

"Running, mostly. I go for a five-mile run every morning before I come to work—or at least I try to."

"And you, Axel?"

He now sat on the other side of the table, to her right. He hadn't spoken yet, but her body tensed in anticipation of the sound of his voice.

"I shoot pool and play basketball. I also like working with my hands."

Her gaze dropped to his hands. They were big, with long fingers, which he'd stroked over her skin with utmost skill, and fisted in her hair as he bent her over the arm of the sofa in his room.

Naphressa shifted in the chair, fighting back the dirty thoughts that seemed to want to take control of her brain.

"You do woodwork?" Zeke asked.

"Not exactly. I like to build things. For instance, over a year ago I was in Belize on vacation and volunteered for a week to help build a school while I was there."

She glanced up, expecting to meet his eyes but was disappointed when all his attention was focused on Zeke.

"You're a nice guy," Zeke said. "When I go on vacation, all I want to do is lay out in the sun and get a tan. And eat more than I should."

The others laughed, while a faint smile crossed Axel's lips. His attention finally gravitated to her and she couldn't look away.

"I think we're about ready to wrap up?" Anton looked around the room. "All we need to do is get everyone to sign on the dotted line."

There was a series of nods and papers were passed around like plates at Sunday dinner. The contracts were signed and a date and time was established for Anton and Jen to do an onsite follow-up in a couple of days. Finally, the group filtered out, leaving Naphressa, Zeke, and Axel behind. Zeke kept busy gathering up folders and documents. Axel approached where Naphressa stood at the refreshment cart, trying to decide if she wanted to steal a donut for the ride home. She snacked a lot—donuts, chips, popcorn. Lucky for her, she didn't gain weight easily.

As Axel neared, the *thump-thump* of her heart hitting against her breastbone made breathing extremely difficult.

"It was good seeing you again," he said in a low voice.

"Yes, you too."

He didn't move. He kept staring at her. His gaze poured over her body in such a way that if Zeke had been paying attention, he'd know without a doubt there was a salacious history between them.

"I thought...nothing. Take care." Axel turned abruptly, said goodbye to Zeke, and left the room.

Naphressa's lungs deflated—a bit from relief, a bit from disappointment. What did she expect? She had not only been very clear that she wasn't going to get involved with him, she was still wearing her wedding ring.

"Ready?" Zeke's hands were filled with their work product.

"Ready."

Naphressa flashed a smile and followed him out the door. She looked up and down the hall but saw no sign of Axel. He was long gone. It was better this way. They needed to keep their distance from each other, because the sparks of desire were very much alive.

Axel Becker was dark and tempting, like some decadent treat she craved but knew better than to indulge in again because he was absolutely no good for her. He could throw all her plans askew.

She couldn't risk getting close to him again because she had too much to lose.

4

Once safely ensconced in her car, Naphressa dialed her sister's number on the Bluetooth.

"Hello." Hazel's voice came through the speakers sounding breathless and harried. Not surprising, with a crying baby in the background.

"I need to talk. Is this a good time?" Naphressa asked.

"No, but I need a break. Give me a minute while I put Regina down. She's working my nerves today. I've said it before, and I'll say it again, my kids should be the cornerstone in a campaign for birth control use. I'm certain I could lower the rate of unwanted pregnancies in this country."

"Gee, where have I heard that before? Regina is your fourth child in eight years, Hazel. Your argument sounds very empty at this point."

"It's Darren's fault. If he weren't so sexy and persuasive, I'd never have another child, I swear. Hang on a sec."

The phone went silent as Hazel put her on mute. The "sec" took three minutes, but when she came back on the line, the sound of a screaming baby had disappeared.

"Whew. Okay, what's up?"

Naphressa sped past a yellow light. "Remember I told you I was going to Abraham, MacKenzie & Wong for a meeting?"

"Yep. You said they're the firm Hayes Realty decided to hire to manage the buyout. Did something go wrong?"

"Not exactly. Guess who's the senior attorney overseeing the project?"

"There's no way I can guess. Who is it?"

"Axel, the man I met in Belize."

"*Whaaat?* No way."

"Yes. What are the chances?"

"Did you have any idea when you saw his name? That's not exactly a common name."

"I never saw his name or heard his name mentioned before today. The firm assigned him at the last minute because the other lead—Simons—got pulled away to a case that's going into litigation. His full name is Axel Becker."

"Wow. Well, do you think you can work with him?"

Naphressa pulled to a stop at a traffic light and let a few seconds pass before she answered. "I can work with him, *but* he's interested in more than work."

"Ah, sookie-sookie now, what does that mean?"

"See, this is why you have four kids. You're always thinking about sex."

Hazel belted out a loud laugh. "Like you're not. Leave me alone and answer the question."

Naphressa pulled away from the light and eased her car into the line at a Burger King drive-thru. "Yes, I can work with him, but he definitely wants more. He pretty much told me so."

"What are you going to do?"

"Nothing. I think I made it clear that we can't rekindle what happened in Belize. First of all, it would be unprofessional for us to get involved. I'm his client. He's my attorney. But even more than that, I...I can't allow Victor and Kathy to get a hint that there's another man in my life."

"Nessa, your husband is dead."

"I know, but I work for his family. I can't move on with my life while I'm there. I can't flaunt my new relationship, and I intend to stay with Hayes Realty for a while."

Her sister sighed heavily, full disapproval evident on the line. "I'm not going to lecture you anymore. You know how I feel, and it's your decision, but I don't think you need them."

"I don't *need* them, but I'm not ready to go yet. Besides, Byron was a hero. A certain period of mourning is expected."

"You weren't worried about mourning when you were under Mr. Corporate Attorney in Belize," Hazel said dryly.

"That's different. I was overseas."

"Oh, that's right. I forgot, only domestic dick counts."

"I hate you."

Giggling because she'd tickled herself way too much, Hazel said, "Sis, all I'm saying is your life doesn't have to come to a standstill. You're young, only thirty-two years old. You should get out there and date and enjoy yourself, even if it's not with Axel. You know what, never mind. We've had this conversation before, and I said no more lectures. Scratch that, one more thing. You—"

"Two seconds ago you said no more lectures," Naphressa bluntly reminded her sister.

"One more teeny-tiny piece of advice that I have to give you. Actually, it's not teeny-tiny. It's huge."

"Fine. I'm listening." She tapped her fingers on the steering wheel.

"You don't owe Byron's family anything. You're good at your job, and they should be happy to have you. Hell, you were the one who got them the Brixton deal."

"I was at a conference that *they* sent me to."

"Be that as it may, your networking got you the scoop. You found out Brixton was going bankrupt, ran the numbers, and presented the project to Victor and he loved it. Furthermore, you don't owe the memory of Byron any loyalty. What he did was wonderful and brave, but unfortunately, it cost him his life. That doesn't mean you have to stay true to him, especially after how he treated you. Take the ring off and move on."

"Move on where?" Naphressa demanded.

"Find another job."

She gnawed on a corner of her lip. Once she completed this project, she'd have a better shot at securing her future. "Not yet. Maybe when this project is over. It's the biggest of my career."

"I hope it's not too late by then."

Her confidence taking a hit, Naphressa slumped in the car seat. "Maybe too late for Axel, but there'll be other men, right?"

"There hasn't been anyone since him, except for that hookup with the guy you met online. You dumped him pretty quickly. Your words were, and I quote, 'He's not Axel.' End quote."

Naphressa glanced around the parking lot filled with cars as people rolled in and out picking up fast-food meals at the end of the day. No, he hadn't been Axel, but she couldn't have Axel.

She had so many regrets from her years with Byron, and if she could go back in time, she'd behave differently. But she had life better than most and couldn't jeopardize it now. She had to hold this deal together, not only for herself, but for all the people on The Brixton Group staff she now felt responsible for. She'd literally be saving jobs with this buyout and intended to see it through to the end.

"I got this. I know what I'm doing," she said, affecting way more confidence than she felt.

AXEL WALKED into his house from the garage and absentmindedly tossed his keys onto the counter. This was the house Rose had wanted, and while he liked it, he played with the idea of selling it and getting something smaller like a condo.

He grabbed a bottle of beer from the fridge and sipped it as he strolled into the den and fed the fish he hadn't even wanted. Rose had planned to toss them out when she moved to Maryland, but he'd felt sorry for the little guys and set them up on a table in a large tank. He'd named them Goldie and Red. Nothing fancy—just names that matched their color.

Byron Hayes.

That name had been on his mind since the office. He was now in a position to do a little digging into Naphressa's deceased husband. What did she mean he was a hero?

He sat down in his home office and immediately went online. After a few minutes, he found an article that gave a comprehensive recounting of Byron's death.

Skimming the article, he learned that Byron Hayes was only thirty-three years old when he passed in a fire. Flames engulfed an apartment building his family owned, and he happened to be there the same day inspecting the property and meeting with the onsite staff.

Before the firefighters arrived, Byron had selflessly rushed into the burning building and rescued a dog, two kids, and their grandfather from one of the apartments. He'd gone in a second time to save an elderly woman trapped in a studio in the back. Unfortunately, neither Byron nor the woman came out alive. He died a hero, having given his life to save others.

Axel placed his beer on the desk in front of him. Byron was a good-looking guy, brown-skinned with a big, white-toothed smile. He looked like a nice guy and had that polished appearance some rich people wore. In the photo, his shirt was neatly pressed, his hair cut short, and his face worry-free. No doubt he had little to worry about. His family was worth tens of millions, and the buyout of the smaller real estate firm and all its holdings at such a bargain would significantly increase their port-folio and net worth.

In one photo, there were flowers, teddy bears, and other memorabilia outside the building where the fire took place. There was also a photo of him and his parents, and another showed him cutting the ribbon on a newly built commercial building on the south end of town.

One smaller photo was of him and Naphressa, arms around each other, smiling. The caption said the photo was from their honeymoon in Mexico.

Axel abruptly stopped rocking in the chair and took another look at the date of the fire.

"Hold up," he muttered.

The fire had taken place five months *after* he and Naphressa met in Belize. That would mean...

Axel's eyes zeroed in on the date again. He couldn't believe what he was seeing. During those five days and four nights they spent together—making love like the world would end the next day—she'd been married to Byron Hayes.

5

He didn't need to be here, yet here he was, micromanaging a project that could run smoothly without him, and using this meeting as an excuse to see Naphressa again.

Only minutes before, they'd come back from visiting the complex that had sent The Brixton Group spiraling into financial ruin. The outside of the main building looked neat and stable, but inside major renovations were underway—or at least had been until the company ran out of money.

Standing in a corner of the conference room where Anton, Jen, and several members of the Hayes Realty staff had convened after the visit, Axel sipped chilled water from a glass and observed Naphressa.

She stood before the group, speaking in clear measured tones, responding to questions with an incredible knowledge of not only the deal but the company they were going to absorb. She was impressive, and as he listened to her talk, that made him want to spend more time with her, but if he intended to work on changing her mind, he needed answers to his questions.

Her marriage couldn't have shocked him more if he'd been told she was an alien from another planet. He'd imagined seeing her again, kissing that sexy smirk from her lips, and reliving the magic they'd experienced overseas. And maybe doing something really crazy, like eventually giving her a ring. Except she already had a ring.

But she hadn't been wearing a ring when they met, so what prompted her to take it off? The need for freedom like she had expressed? And if so, what prompted her to put it back on? Guilt at what she'd done, or was she not completely over her dead husband?

Dark eyes that seemed bottomless in depth met his, and he wondered if there were other secrets, besides being married, that she'd kept from him.

"We're going to expand these buildings and leave the exterior of the main building mostly as is, with only a few minor changes. Victor has very specific ideas in mind for the interior design," Naphressa said.

With a laser pointer, she drew an invisible circle around areas for improvement on a big screen that showed the altered renovation plans. Her curly black hair was pulled into a tight bun, but he knew what it felt like to have the thick tendrils brush across his palm, and to tighten his fingers in their soft depths as he plunged his body deeply into hers.

The forest-green skirt she wore stretched over her hips, and the matching jacket enveloped her curves like a tight but comfortable squeeze. Enough to show off her gorgeous figure, but not too much as to seem inappropriate for work. Meanwhile, tan heels transformed her ankles and calves into the sexiest arch he'd ever seen on a woman.

Axel shifted his weight from one foot to the other, restless and anxious to talk to her privately. The opportunity finally came thirty minutes later when the meeting adjourned.

Everyone started packing up their note pads and pens while Naphressa slipped from the room.

"You going back to the office?" Anton asked Axel.

He shook his head. "No, I'm going to stop at Naphressa's office for a few minutes. I need to talk to her about something. I'll catch up with you later."

"A'ight. Later."

Naphressa tossed her jacket on the visitor chair and fell into the brown leather chair behind her desk. She rotated her shoulders and rolled her neck. She hadn't expected to see Axel today, and having him in the room had made her extremely tense.

The phone on her desk rang.

"Hello?"

Loretta's southern twang came through. "Axel Becker would like a moment with you. Should I send him in?"

Her first instinct was to say she was unavailable because she didn't want to be alone, in private with him.

Instead, she said, "Yes, send him in." Might as well get this over with.

The door opened and he strolled in. Well over six feet, he had a great walk and owned any room he entered. That's how he'd entered the assembly room at the site in Belize, planted his feet wide, and assessed the area as if he were the one in charge of the whole operation and not simply a volunteer like everyone else.

Naphressa watched that same captivating walk now, which made her stomach muscles tremble in time to each step. His presence in her office put her on edge, heightening the already nervous energy that had been present since his unexpected appearance earlier at the building site.

She stood and kept the desk between them as a barrier. "Hi. Can I help you?"

"I came to see your paintings. Thought I could check them out before I left."

"They're on the wall." She strolled over to the collage of six by nine watercolors. Ten of them, each one of a building or landscape. "These are all building renovations I've worked on since I've been in this position, and the landscapes are various spots around the city that caught my eye," she explained.

"Are these all your paintings?" Axel asked.

"I have others at home and bigger canvases. They're mostly landscapes—beach scenes, meadows, that kind of thing."

She knew the moment he came to stand directly behind her. The air shifted. "Nice," he said in a quiet tone.

Her sex pulsed in respond to the sound of his voice, and she turned slowly, meeting his gaze head on. "You didn't come in here to see my paintings."

"Am I that obvious?"

"I'm afraid so."

His eyes narrowed to slits. "You forgot to mention an important piece of information about your marriage to Byron Hayes. You didn't mention you were married to him when you and I were in Belize."

Uh-oh. Naphressa swallowed hard. "You went digging, I see."

"Wasn't hard to find out when the information about his death is all over the internet."

"What do you want to ask me?"

"Why?" he asked testily, though his expression remained mostly neutral.

She could imagine him negotiating across a table with opposing counsel, just the right amount of steel in his voice to convey the message that they needed to take it or leave it.

"Why did you sleep with me when you were married to another man? I don't go around screwing other men's wives."

She clasped her hands tightly together. "I should have told you."

"No shit."

Naphressa put distance between them, resting her bottom and both hands on the lip of her credenza against the wall. Time to come clean.

"Before he died, Byron and I hit a very rough patch. We were having problems, and no, having sex with you did not help our problems, and I didn't do it expecting to improve our relationship. He and I hadn't seen eye to eye for a long time, and frankly, the turning point came when I found out he was cheating on me."

"He was cheating on *you*?" Axel asked incredulously.

She smiled faintly. "I'll take your surprise as a compliment. Yes, me. I'm not proud of what happened between you and me, but as far as I was concerned, our marriage was over, and I told him so, but..." She sighed, smoothing a hand over her hairline. "He became angry and told me he wasn't ready for me to leave, and if I did leave, not only would I lose my job at Hayes Realty, he would make sure I never worked in Atlanta real estate again. As I'm sure you know, the Hayes family name carries a lot of clout in this city. I was...trapped, I guess you could say."

That wasn't all he'd said that day. He'd lashed out, making it clear that the only reason she held the position as project manager was because of her marriage to him. Her rapid climb up the company ladder hadn't been earned. He was an only child and his parents had had him late in life. They adored him. According to him, they'd granted her those promotions because he asked.

Axel looked at her in a different way now. The anger was gone, and something akin to concern filled his eyes. "He wanted to hold on to you though he was doing his dirt."

"Exactly. He knew I loved my job and chances were, I wasn't going anywhere. That gave him carte blanche to continue sleeping around. He held on to me but never touched me again and didn't bother hiding his affairs anymore. Lipstick on his collar, the scent of perfume in his jacket, openly sexting with other women. The whole bit." She swallowed back the resurgence of the pain and humiliation she'd endured for that year. "We portrayed a happily married couple to his family, friends, and business associates. Meanwhile, he was coming in all hours of the morning after staying out all night. The trip to Belize was a gift to myself—something to make me feel better." She shrugged. "Just an escape for a little while. But then...then I met you, and the trip turned into a little more."

"Much more, wouldn't you say?"

"Axel, please..." she breathed.

The muscle in his right jaw flexed. "Hearing you say my name like that brings back so many memories. I haven't been able to get you out of my head. I wanted to see you again. I thought that's what you wanted, too."

"I did, I do, to some degree, but the situation I'm in is tough. Byron's family still sees me as married to him."

"That's ridiculous."

"It's the truth."

"Do *you* see yourself as still married?"

"No," Naphressa answered with a vigorous head shake. "That married feeling died a long time ago when I found out about Byron's infidelities, and certainly when he didn't stop sleeping around. He didn't want to fix our marriage, and maybe that was the worst blow of all. He more or less told me he married me to keep his parents from nagging him about getting married. I was the fool who believed our marriage was built on love and companionship." She shook her head in disgust, the twist of pain making her upper lip twitch.

During that difficult period, she'd also learned that he'd put her off on having children for the same reason—he didn't really want to be married in the first place. He used her as a convenient excuse to get his parents off his back and prove he was a responsible person, while he continued to live a bachelor lifestyle.

"He wasn't all bad, of course. That was the crazy thing about Byron. He had his moments. He was always full of compliments and had adoring eyes that made me feel as if he didn't have eyes for anyone else. He also had a big heart. He just didn't want a wife."

"You deserved better. That should have never happened to you," Axel bit out.

"Life goes on. It's not the end of the world, and despite all that happened, I had my job that I loved," Naphressa said, putting on a brave front though her heart ached for a better type of relationship. A healthy one, consisting of mutual love and respect.

"It's not the end the world, but what if you could have something better? Our time at that resort was like paradise to me, and I haven't stopped thinking about you since I saw you at the firm. Hell, who am I kidding? I haven't stopped thinking about you since you left me in Belize."

"I'm not looking for another husband. The first time didn't work out too well for me," Naphressa said evenly.

"Did you enjoy your time with me?"

They'd laughed and made love like a couple who'd been together for years. Working with him at the school for those two days—lugging bricks and pounding nails—had been enjoyable because *he'd* been there.

"Yes."

"Do you want to relive paradise?"

More than anything. "Yes."

"And you admit the sex was amazing?" A corner of his mouth quirked upward.

Her nipples perked up and tightened, and she couldn't help but respond with a small smile of her own. "There's no denying that."

"Then let's have sex."

"Excuse me?'

"You heard me. Name your stipulations, because I know you have some since you don't want your former in-laws to find out you're seeing a new man. I'll agree to anything you ask if it means I get to fuck you again."

Oh my. Her mouth fell open. "That's...blunt."

"I don't like to beat around the bush."

The heat pulsing at her core matched the raging inferno in his eyes.

"You're serious?"

"Never been more serious in my life."

The tension in the room crackled. "Just sex?"

There was a moment of hesitation, as if he didn't want to agree with her and planned to talk her out of the idea. "If that's all you'll give me," he finally said.

Naphressa's fingers tightened on the edge of the credenza as she tossed around his crazy idea. "Once a week." She didn't think she could handle more time than that with him. She'd become too attached.

"What else?"

"That's it."

"What day?" He came closer, eyes never leaving hers.

She couldn't move, imprisoned without a single one of his fingers touching her.

"Fridays." She whispered the first day that popped into her head.

Axel's head tilted to the side, and a slow smile came over his face. "Today is Friday."

6

Naphressa knew where he was going before he said the words. That arrogant, knowing smile and the way the heat in his eyes torched her skin hinted at the words that would issue from his mouth.

That's why she stepped into him, lips already parted in offer. No words, only actions and the sounds of their heated breaths blowing out in anticipation. She wanted this as much as he did, and he'd given her the perfect excuse to forego propriety and give in to her basic instincts—lust, desire, the need to be held and caressed like a woman of value instead of someone who didn't deserve to be treated with respect and care.

His lips ground into hers and his rough, passionate kiss made the rest of the world disappear. Her knees quivered at the way he grabbed her bun and tilted back her head to take control of her mouth and seize what she willingly gave. With her pulse roaring in her wrists, Naphressa flattened her body against his, digging her fingers into the firm flesh of his back and grinding her hips into the hardening length at his pelvis.

With an abrupt twist of his hands, Axel forced her to face

the credenza. Her fingers fastened on one of the built-in shelves above her head while she grabbed his hand and covered her right breast through her silk top. He squeezed, and the nipple immediately hardened. She let loose a low moan as she shuddered. Impatiently, Axel yanked open her silk blouse and two buttons popped off to the floor. He cupped her breasts with possessive hands as his mouth fastened on the side of her neck. His warm breath feathered over her as his teeth scraped almost angrily against her skin. His hands were deliciously rough and his hips moved against her bottom in a lewd, erotic grind that had her arching backward and rubbing against him in return.

Naphressa never thought she'd be the kind of woman to have sex in her office, yet here she was, risking her livelihood, everything she'd worked for, for a quick screw in this very office.

The door wasn't locked, and Loretta could do a quick double knock and come in any minute, but she dared not stop Axel. Not now, with his hand under her skirt and between her thighs, shoved low in her panties, fingers stroking her wet clit. His other hand wreaked havoc with her swollen breasts—the firm massage creating a swell of pleasure that threatened to push a cry from her throat.

This was madness, insanity. But she couldn't stop. She needed him as much as she needed her next breath. Biting hard on her lower lip, she fought the urge to release a scream and settled for a low, needy moan instead.

As he hiked her skirt higher, she rested trembling hands atop the smooth wood surface of the credenza. She listened to the ominous sound of him undoing his belt bucket and shimmied out of her panties, tossing them aside. Then there was the sound of his zipper, and a mere second later his hands were on her naked hips. One foot slid between hers and shoved her legs wider. She whimpered, her wet core throbbing and ready for his possession.

With a low grunt, Axel was inside her. Wide. Deep. Nothing but complete satisfaction as he filled her. Her head fell forward, and she pushed back against him, curling her spine.

Fingers spread out on the credenza top, her breathing became labored. "Yes, yes," she panted as he plowed into her, each thrust taking her closer to bliss. "Yes!"

The loud shout filled the office, and Axel's big hand swiftly covered her mouth.

"I've dreamed of this," he rasped in her ear, never breaking stride.

Naphressa had dreamed of this, too, and fantasized about running into him again. Reality was so much better than her dreams.

Dizzying pleasure tore through her body as the orgasm burst free. Tears filled her eyes and she squeezed them shut, half-moaning, half-screaming behind the giant palm that covered her mouth and kept co-workers from rushing into the room out of concern.

"You ruined my blouse."

"My bad." Several feet away, Axel zipped his pants, keeping an eye on her. A self-satisfied smile curled his lips at the corners.

"Yeah, you look real sorry," Naphressa said, picking up the two pearl buttons from the floor.

She set them on the desk and pulled the edges of her blouse together. It wasn't really ruined. She just needed to sew back on the buttons.

She moved to walk past Axel, but he took her by the upper arm and pulled her into his chest. His mouth lowered to hers and she sighed against his lips. Their first kiss had been out-of-control fireworks that demanded capitulation. This one was calmer and more of a seduction. She melted against him, nipples pebbling again when they came into contact with his hard chest.

Axel's hands smoothed over her lower back and came to rest on her bottom. He gently kissed the corners of her mouth before lifting his head to gaze down into her eyes.

"Even better than I remembered," he whispered.

"Me, too," Naphressa admitted.

His mouth lowered to hers again, and they engaged in a leisurely kiss before she eased away and picked up her jacket to cover her top. Lucky for her, since a double knock sounded at the door and Loretta walked in.

She and Axel froze, Naphressa only managing to close the last button on her jacket seconds before, and Axel shifted his gaze, which had been filled with longing as if he'd wanted to reopen the jacket and have another go at her breasts.

"Excuse me for interrupting, darlin', but I knew you wanted the plans for the building on Cape Street." Loretta handed Naphressa a pile of papers as Axel watched in silence.

"I did. Thanks."

With a quick smile at them both, Loretta exited and left them alone again.

Naphressa let out a loud breath of relief but remained concerned. Did Loretta notice the faint musky scent that remained in the air? Did she recognize it as Naphressa having had her back blown out by the guest in her office?

"Shit." She dropped the papers onto the credenza.

"She doesn't know, and even if she thinks she knows, she has no proof."

"When has anyone ever needed proof for gossip? That was careless and foolish. My job—"

"Is secure."

"No, it's not," Naphressa snapped.

"You're really worried about this?" he asked.

"Yes! You finally get the memo." She rubbed her temple. She couldn't lose everything she'd worked so hard for simply because she was horny. "We can't do that again."

"We won't, but I couldn't resist you, and I've waited a long, long time to see you again."

His soft tread on the carpet made her raise her gaze to his. He stopped before her, and she stiffened. Whatever he had planned, she'd resist him this time. There was too much at stake.

"Fridays, right?" he asked.

"Right," she answered.

He reached behind her and picked up a small notepad and pen. He scribbled something on the pad, tore off the sheet, and then tossed the pad and pen back onto the credenza. He extended the sheet of paper.

Naphressa looked at it. "What's this?"

"My address. Be there next Friday night, bring an overnight bag, and don't wear your ring."

"Just like that? What if I don't show up?"

"You'll show up." He planted a quick, hard kiss on her mouth and started toward the door.

"How can you be so sure?" she called after him.

Axel paused, his gaze scrolling over her in a knowing way. "Because you want this as much as I do." He opened the door and left.

Naphressa pressed her fingertips to her throbbing lips. Damn, he was right.

Arrogant ass.

7

She was really doing this.

Before knocking on Axel's door, Naphressa glanced around the neighborhood, taking stock of the quiet, tree-lined street. Shrubs flanked either side of the stairs leading up to the front door of the two-story home made of stone and brick. It looked like the kind of place a family of four would occupy—not a bachelor arranging weekly sexcapades.

When Axel came to the door, he lifted her left hand to check for the ring, which she'd left at home. He dropped her hand.

"Satisfied?" she asked.

"Yes. Welcome." He took the overnight bag from her shoulder and placed it on the first step of the staircase leading to the second floor.

She half expected him to get down to business immediately. Instead, he showed her around the first floor, made up of large rooms, including a formal dining room, an office, and a full bathroom. Very neat and without clutter, the design concept was modern with a homey feel that made her want to take off her shoes and curl up on the tan sofa in the living room.

Axel had clearly showered right before her arrival. Water droplets glinted under the light in his damp hair, and the fresh scent of pine soap commingled with the earthy aroma of his cologne. He wore a ribbed cotton long-sleeved shirt with three buttons that stopped mid-chest. Speaking of chest, the soft fabric outlined his perfectly, molding to the contours of his hard pecs and tempting her to touch. Combined with a pair of dark slacks that flattered his tall frame and thick thighs, the man was a delectable tease, making her almost pant in anticipation for the night to come.

Naphressa paused in the open doorway of the kitchen. "I didn't expect all this," she said, walking in and gesturing at the set table.

"What did you think? That I'd bumrush you at the door and tear your clothes off?"

She laughed, licking her dry lips. "Nothing quite so barbaric."

"But close," he said with a hint of a smile around his eyes.

"Yes. After all, we both know why I'm here."

"Yeah, and I'm struggling to keep my hands to myself right now."

Naphressa took the compliment in stride, her walk a little more confident as she strolled to the table. It was set with covered dishes and white plates with a gold strip around the circumference. Fresh cut tulips sat in a glass vase, and the scent of roasted meat perfumed the air.

"But," he added, "I decided I better feed you. I hope you haven't eaten."

"Only a light snack."

"Good. Have a seat and eat as much as you like." As she settled in the soft chair, he bent to her ear. "You'll need the calories for the long night ahead."

The back of his fingers touched the side of her neck ever so slightly. His touch was sensual and already way too familiar.

She drew in an involuntary breath, her stomach contracting with need.

"A man who can cook in the bedroom and in the kitchen. You're like a unicorn. That's very rare," she remarked.

"Not as rare as you think, but I'll take the compliment. Wine?" He held up a bottle of Sauvignon blanc.

She shook her head. "Water, if you have it."

"I do." He filled a glass. "I remember you didn't drink in Belize, either. Mind if I ask why?"

"Not at all. I don't like the taste of alcoholic beverages."

"I can understand that."

She sipped her water, watching him sit across from her and spread a white napkin across his thighs. "What is all this, Axel?"

He looked up. "What do you mean?"

"I mean, all this." She made a sweeping gesture with one hand. "Wine, a home-cooked meal. I thought I was coming here to have sex."

"Can't wait, can you?"

She glared at him and he laughed.

"We will have sex, but like I said, I need to feed you first. Later, we'll burn off all those calories." He flashed a sexy grin, his teeth looking especially white and brilliant because they were surrounded by the black hairs of his groomed beard and mustache.

He lifted the dome off a serving dish with a flourish and revealed a cut up roasted chicken dribbled with gravy. "Chicken and roasted potatoes. I hope you like rosemary." He lifted the glass cover off a white bowl and then off a large wooden bowl. "And a fresh salad, tossed with my own honey, lime, and garlic dressing."

"You're going to spoil me."

"I hope so. *Bon appetit.*"

If he went to all this trouble for a woman he only wanted to screw, how did he behave when he was in love, when a woman received his devotion and attention? Was Axel the kind to stay loyal and respect his vows, or would he turn into a fraud like her ex?

There was no way to know for sure, but right now, he was doing a helluva good job convincing her he was husband material.

THE MEAL HAD BEEN GREAT, the conversation flowed smoothly, and Naphressa had a wicked sense of humor that kept him laughing throughout dinner.

Seated on the futon in his office with an after-dinner drink of rum and Coke in the hand resting on his knee, Axel's eyes followed her as she glided across the carpet, gaze trained on the various trophies he'd won in basketball leagues with his friends Cole and Braxton. There were other awards, too—including one for community service and a humanitarian award given by the mayor for Axel's work with the homeless.

"You've done a lot of good in the community," she said, leaning closer to read the words on one of the certificates.

"I try."

Standing across the room, her eyes found his. "Don't be modest. All of these awards suggest you do a lot more than try. You're rolling up your sleeves and putting in the work."

"My parents ran a nonprofit for years, before they finally had to let it go because they couldn't raise the funds necessary to keep the company afloat. I worked there off and on over the years, and I guess the desire to do more stuck with me. It's rewarding work."

"Is that why you ended up in Belize building a school while on vacation?"

"You could say that. I hadn't planned to, but a member of

the resort staff offhandedly mentioned they needed help at the school, and I wanted to help. Why did you participate?" He sipped his drink.

"Because you asked. But Belize was a spur-of-the-moment trip. I picked a place on the map and bought a ticket to escape."

"Lucky for me."

"Lucky for us both, I guess," she said softly. Her eyes turned thoughtful. "Have you ever been married, Axel?"

"Never got that far, but I was engaged once."

"What happened?"

"Trying to understand me?" he asked, shifting on the futon.

"Maybe. I feel like you know a lot about me, but I know very little about you. Why didn't you make it to the altar?"

"Long story short, Rose, my fiancée, broke off our engagement."

Her eyebrows flew higher. "*She* ended your engagement? Why?"

He laughed. "Now it's my turn to take your surprise as a compliment. She got a job offer she couldn't refuse and left the state."

Naphressa rested a hip against his desk. "Do you keep in touch?"

"Nah. We did for a while, but after about a year, the calls fell off. I got a text from her for my birthday two years ago. Haven't heard from her since."

"How long ago did you split?"

"Four years this summer. How long were you and Byron married?"

"Five years. I was twenty-five when we met, still trying to figure out what to do with myself. I was a property manager at one of his parents' apartment complexes. He came on site and did an inspection and we chatted, went to lunch. I didn't think much about our interaction. I thought he was handsome and funny, but that's it. I didn't think he'd even noticed me. Two days later he called and asked me out on a date. I surprised myself by saying yes."

"Surprised yourself?"

"I don't think it's a good idea to mix business and pleasure." She bit the corner of her mouth, eyes becoming heavy-lidded. "I've had a hard time sticking to that ideal, it seems."

"I think you're allowed to make exceptions. In my case, anyway."

"Only in your case?" she said with a smile and one elevated eyebrow.

"Yes."

His chest tightened as he continued to look at her. The dark jeans and off-the-shoulder pink blouse showed off the beauty of her dark brown complexion and all night had been tempting him to touch his lips to her skin.

"You're a beautiful woman, you know that?" he asked, letting his gaze scroll down her figure.

"So I've been told."

"So it's not news to you."

"Not at all," she said loftily with an easy smile.

A few seconds ticked by. "Come here."

He wanted to kiss her. Seven days had passed since he'd had the pleasure, but her taste was fresh on his lips. He could hardly wait to experience every inch of her naked skin against his when their bodies joined together again.

She set her glass of water on the table. Her chin tilted higher, eyes darkening as she approached and stopped a foot out of reach.

He looked her steadily in the eyes. "Undress for me."

She seemed to hesitate for a minute. Unsure. Studying him. Then she unsnapped her jeans and pushed them down her thighs. She stepped out of her shoes and tossed the jeans to the floor. Next came the pink top, pulled over her head and dropped atop the jeans. A pink demi-cup bra covered her full breasts and matching lace panties covered the lower part of her body. She was all feminine curves and smooth, dusky-dark skin.

"All of it," he said throatily, temperature rising as he watched her.

She smirked at him, the same smile that she'd shot at him numerous times during their trip. He liked her confidence. She was sexy personified.

She stood before him, totally nude, and he wished he could freeze this moment in time—this feeling of complete and utter satisfaction. This was the woman he'd been looking for, but how to convince her that he was the man she'd been looking for?

Axel lowered to his knees and kissed the trimmed triangle between her thighs. He flicked his tongue along her damp slit and groaned. As he continued to taste, she steadied herself with her hands on his head. Angling her hips, she pushed farther into his mouth.

But he refused to go deeper, laughing softly at her frustrated whine.

"Please, Axel." Her voice trembled with desire.

He decided to show mercy and lifted her from the floor. With long strides, he took her to his bedroom and laid her across the bed. He stripped out of his clothes and then lowered his head between her legs again. His mouth simply hadn't had enough, and he loved her taste. She cried out at the renewed contact and sent a shiver rippling down the center of his back.

He planted gentle, hot kisses all over her sex. When she came, her honey dripped onto his tongue, and he greedily licked every drop from her swollen flesh.

He kissed his way up her lean torso and passed his tongue across her left nipple. She crushed his head to her, her moans filling the dark room as she smoothed her hands over his head in encouraging strokes.

Minutes later, he joined their bodies with a smooth slide between her thighs. Huffing at his thrusting hips, she clawed his shoulders and begged for another release.

His lips were on her arched throat, his hands gripping her soft bottom as he fucked her slow and steady, taking his time to savor the sweet, tight clasp of her sex around his dick.

"You feel so damn good," he groaned.

"Yes, yes," she hissed, breaths coming faster and her chin tilting higher toward the ceiling.

He felt the moment she came, her feminine muscles convulsing around him in rapid-fire motion. He barely had a moment to take a breath before he lost all control and pounded faster, spilling into the condom and winding his arms around her so tight he immediately let go for fear he'd crushed her.

Seconds later, their breathing slowly returning to normal, Axel held Naphressa in the prison of his arms so she couldn't move and kissed her damp forehead.

Then he finally succumbed to sleep.

8

Following the tempting aroma of bacon and freshly brewed coffee, Naphressa sauntered along the downstairs hallway, stretching and yawning as she went. She should have left first thing this morning but couldn't bring herself to leave the warm comfort of Axel's bed and arms, only getting up ten minutes ago because *he'd* left and she missed cuddling with him.

She entered the kitchen where he was busy at the stove. He didn't hear her enter, so she was able to watch him for a bit. He wore his pajama bottoms but no shirt, whistling softly to himself as he made pancakes to go along with the bacon draining on paper towels in a plate on the counter. With great difficulty she refrained from rubbing her face against the soft skin of his muscular back.

"Good morning," she said, padding over to the coffee pot.

He glanced up and flashed her a pristine smile that brightened his face. Ugh, he was perfect, and the way his dark eyes scrolled down her body—adorned only in a white sleeveless tee and white panties—made her lady parts throb at the memory of how his lips had turned her inside out last night.

"Good morning," he replied.

Naphressa prepared her coffee with a little sugar and then leaned a hip against the counter as she watched him pour pancake batter into a hot skillet.

"You're too good to be true."

He arched an eyebrow at her. "You don't really believe that."

"I do. Look at you. You're shirtless and making pancakes from scratch, for goodness sake."

He laughed and continued working. "They're not from scratch. They're from a box, and all I had to do was add water."

"But I bet you could make them from scratch."

"I can," he confirmed with a slick smile.

Naphressa glanced around the spacious kitchen, complete with a smart refrigerator, double ovens, and a small island in the center. Natural light poured through the curtainless windows, brightened the opened space, and sent an invitation to come outdoors and enjoy the deck and large, sloping back yard.

"You get so much light in this house. It would be great for painting."

"Any time you want to set up an easel and paint, you're welcome to do it. The den would be a good spot." He nodded at the space that opened into the kitchen.

She didn't respond, not daring to read too much into the invitation.

"It was a suggestion, nothing more. Don't overthink it."

"I'm not," she insisted.

"Uh-huh. I saw the wheels turning."

"You think you know everything."

"That's because I do. I didn't tell you? I'm a mind reader."

"What am I thinking right now?" She stared at him.

He narrowed his eyes, pretending to concentrate. "You're thinking...I can't wait to get this man back into bed."

She guffawed, the sound of her exaggerated laughter filling the room.

"I'm not wrong," he said.

"You're dead wrong."

He used the spatula to place a pancake on a plate and then poured in the last bit of batter to fry. "Sure. Don't worry, I'll take care of you when I get finished with this food."

"I want to eat when you get finished, thank you very much. Then I'm leaving."

"I was hoping you'd stick around for a while."

"And do what?"

He shrugged. "Talk. Keep me company."

"You don't have anything to do today?"

"No. You?"

"I was going to head over to my sister's for a little bit and watch the kids while she and her husband go out for lunch." Naphressa cradled the mug and sipped her coffee.

"You help them like that a lot?"

"Every now and again, to give them a break. Hazel, my sister, usually has a babysitter, but I offered to do it for her so I'd get to spend time with my niece and nephews."

"So the lady likes kids."

"I like my niece and nephews," she corrected.

"Like I said. You like kids."

She laughed softly. "How about you? Do you like kids?"

"I do. I'm an only child, so I always wanted a big family." He flipped the pancake.

"That explains it."

"Explains what?"

"You're an only child, so that explains why you're so cocky and full of yourself. You experienced a lot of love and attention from doting parents, no doubt."

"You got me, it's true. And I'm really close with my parents, too. They live in Augusta, and I visit them sometimes on the weekends. They have a great marriage. Watching them love on each other after so many years is kind of...refreshing, you know?"

Naphressa stared down into her coffee. "No, I wouldn't know. My parents didn't have the best relationship. It was not ideal in any way. My father was...difficult."

"Difficult how?"

She wondered if she'd said too much. It wasn't easy for her to share such personal information with someone else, and she was more hesitant to do so after listening to how great his parents' marriage was.

"My dad used to belittle my mom. She didn't work outside the home, and she wasn't traditionally smart—you know, with book sense. But she had plenty of common sense and a razor-sharp memory. She knew the price of every grocery item, knew when items would be on sale, comparison shopped and did extreme couponing with the best of them."

"Sounds like she was an amazing woman."

"She was." A lump lodged in her throat and kept Naphressa from speaking for a while. "She died when I was in my twenties, and I regret never telling her how proud I was of her. I learned a lot from watching how she managed our household and saved my father money, but he never appreciated it or acknowledged her contributions."

Axel removed the last pancake and placed it on the plate with the first one. Then he braced his arms on the counter, muscles flexed taut as he watched her sideways. "I bet she knew what you thought."

"I hope so."

He came over and removed the cup from her hands. He set it on the counter and his arms rounded her waist.

"Your dad still alive?"

"No. He passed away a few months after she did." Naphressa smoothed her palms up the biceps on both of his arms. "I hope you know how lucky you are to have both your parents and to have seen them in a healthy relationship."

"Believe me, I know how lucky I am. Seeing them like that helped to influence my beliefs about relationships and marriage. I'm going to be honest with you, since Rose, I haven't been serious about a woman. I've sort of...dated a lot."

"So you're a playboy?"

"I wouldn't say all that. But I've had my fun, and I'm ready to settle down."

"Settling down is a very serious decision to make."

"Yeah, I know." He paused. "I know we said that we would only meet on Fridays, but I want you to consider seeing me outside of Friday nights."

She tensed. "I don't think that's a good idea."

His voice lowered. "Think about it. I'm not pushing, I promise, but I want you to think about it."

She nodded, albeit reluctantly. Her reluctance to spend more time with Axel wasn't only because of Byron's parents. She also worried that any more time and she'd easily fall hard for his charming, sexy self. She wasn't ready for a serious relationship yet. She had a lot on her plate and more she wanted to accomplish, career-wise.

"I'll think about it." She looped her arms around his neck. "You know what?" she said, dropping her voice low.

"What?" He looked at her from beneath heavy lids, pulling her tighter into his warm embrace.

Naphressa stood on her toes. "We need to postpone breakfast for a bit."

"But I slaved over a hot stove all morning," he murmured, bending his head to hers.

"I know, and although I was hungry a few minutes ago, the hunger I'm feeling right now is not for food. You were right. I do want to take you back to bed."

"Oh yeah?" He started walking her backward.

"Yep."

She hopped up into his arms and wrapped her legs around his waist. He was already hard, and her breathing became jagged at the thought of their bodies binding together again. They'd made love twice last night and it wasn't enough.

"Only one thing can fill me up," she whispered in his ear.

"What's that?" He lightly kissed the underside of her jaw and sent tingles scurrying across her skin.

"Your dick."

With a low growl, he rushed out of the kitchen, their full breakfast temporarily forgotten.

9

Axel slid between Braxton and a redheaded guy on the other team. With stealth-like quickness, he stole the ball from a tall, lanky Black guy on the opposing team. Angry shouts followed him as raced down the court, dribbling the ball. Five men's feet stomping behind him like horse's hooves sounded loud in his ears as they clamored after him, but he focused on the destination. As he neared the basket, he jumped high and slammed the ball into the net.

Landing on his feet, he twisted in a one-eighty turn and beat his chest. "Boom! That's game, bitches!"

Roaring with excitement, Cole and Braxton pounded his back and shoulders. The other guys, breathing hard to catch their breaths, glared at them.

"Now what?" Axel yelled, puffing out his chest.

Dunking on them gave him immense satisfaction because they had talked so much trash before the game started.

"Men, fuck you!" The Black guy shot him two birds. "Next time, we'll beat your ass."

"Heard that before. Next time, don't write a check that your ass can't cash," Axel shot back.

The opposing team's other two members were red-faced and shaking with rage. They had no idea who they were up against when they issued the three-on-three challenge to Axel and his boys.

Their opponents sauntered off. Demonstrating poor sportsmanship, they didn't shake hands before they left. As Axel followed his friends over to the bleachers, spattered applause filled the large gym from some of the spectators who had watched the game.

They sat down, and Axel took a clean rag from his bag and mopped the sweat from his brow.

"You talk so much shit," Braxton said, sitting two rows below him.

"*They* talked so much shit and couldn't back it up. Next time I bet their asses will be a little more respectful when they issue a challenge."

Pick-up games at the gym weren't unusual, and neither was some good-natured ribbing among the men and women who came through and played. Axel, Braxton, and Cole were known for wiping the floor with opponents during their normal three-on-three games. Not only did they play well, they'd won trophies at leagues around the city. Over the few years they'd known each other, they'd learned each other's strengths and easily communicated without words, using a simple nod or eye contact.

What *was* unusual was the nasty attitude of the men who'd left, who heard about Axel, Braxton, and Cole's reputation and decided they would be the ones to humble them. Instead, they'd been humbled, and giving them a spanking and sending them away with their tails between their legs made today's win particularly satisfactory.

Axel tossed back his head and swallowed two large gulps of Gatorade.

"Great game, guys." Linda, one of the trainers, stopped in

front of them in a pair of tight black shorts and a black sleeve-less top. The outfit showed off her great body while a short, tapered haircut showed off an attractive face with high cheek-bones and full lips.

"Thanks," Cole said, seated a few feet away on the same row of bleachers as Axel.

"Axel, you got pretty high there at the end. I can't believe you never played professional ball." She didn't bother pretending she was talking to the three of them anymore. Her eyes devoured Axel like a hungry lioness right before she sank her teeth into an antelope's neck.

"Only played in high school and that's it, but I've always loved the game." He kept his voice neutral, not wanting to convey interest in her when there wasn't any.

"I can tell. You looked great out there, as usual. See you later, fellas." She waved and sauntered away with a hip-swinging walk that turned the heads of two men who jogged onto the court from the opposite direction.

Once she was out of earshot, Braxton turned around to him. "Are you ever going to give her another shot? I'm starting to feel sorry for her."

Axel laughed. "Don't. She's a beautiful woman and doesn't have a shortage of admirers clamoring for her attention."

"But she wants you."

"She wants me because she can't have me."

"Anymore," Cole added.

Axel didn't argue. He and Linda had gone out a few times and slept together, but he'd never experienced the connection with her that he longed for. Not like he did with Naphressa.

Braxton stood and stretched. "I'm starving. About to hit the showers and then head out of here."

"See you later, man," Axel said, giving him some dap.

"Later," Cole said. He and Braxton fist-bumped.

Braxton was out of the gym before either of them spoke again.

"You figured out what to get him for his birthday yet?" Cole asked.

"Nah. By the way, I don't understand why we're having a surprise birthday party for a man who doesn't like surprises. Whose idea was that again?"

"Not mine. His sister thought it was a good idea. So you're coming to the party, even though your Friday nights are occupied now?" Cole took a swig from his bottled water.

"Yeah, I'll be there."

"Is Naphressa coming? That'll give us a chance to finally meet this mystery woman. After all, sounds like things are serious between you two since you have a standing Friday night appointment."

"Maybe not serious, but I'm definitely feeling her, and she's feeling me." This morning he'd woken up with her soft body cradled in his arms, her bottom shoved up against his crotch. Once a week was not nearly enough, but he was making do until he could convince her to give him more time.

"So do we get to meet her in a couple of weeks?" Cole asked.

"I doubt it. She's a little gun-shy and has concerns about her dead husband's family seeing us together."

"Are they in the Mafia or something?" Cole asked with a laugh.

Smiling faintly, Axel said, "Nothing so interesting, but let's just say she has concerns that there will be repercussions if they find out she has a new man."

"That's ridiculous."

"That's what I said, but I can't convince her otherwise." He'd tried broaching the subject with her over the phone a few days ago, but she'd once again been adamant there was nothing she could do about the situation now, which had frustrated him.

"Hopefully you can change her mind."

Axel eyed his friend. "Since you're all up in my business, let me ask you something. You bringing Malaya?"

"Thinking about it," Cole replied, a smile breaking out on his face.

"Glad to see that's working out."

"She's a good woman, but she's going through a hard time."

"How so?"

"Her ex-husband's a jerk. He plays games with their daughter, keeping Laya from seeing her. Stuff like that. His family's rich and powerful, so he thinks he can do whatever he likes, but Laya's tired of it and wants full custody."

"Think she has a chance?"

"I believe so," Cole said, his tone grim and jaw tight. "I'll do whatever I can to help her."

"If there's anything I can do, let me know. Family law isn't my area of expertise, but I know plenty of good lawyers who could help. She'll need a good one if her ex's family is a powerful as you say. I know they'll have the best."

"Thanks, I appreciate it. You ready to get out of here?"

"Yeah. Let's go."

They jumped up from the bleachers and exited the gym.

10

They ate dinner on the deck with two portable heaters beside the table because the weather was still too chilly to dine comfortably outside at night. Naphressa enjoyed eating al fresco, with the sounds of the night around them and enough light to see each other clearly yet create an intimate mood.

She could tell something was off with Axel tonight, though, as if he had a lot on his mind. He talked, but was unusually quiet during dinner, letting her do most of the talking. And while he laughed quite a bit, his eyes didn't crinkle in the corners like they usually did. They contained a solemnness, and every so often he looked at her in a way that made her feel as if he was trying to peek inside her soul.

After they cleared the table and he turned on the dishwasher, she came up behind him as he wiped down the counters.

"Domestic men are so sexy," she murmured, wrapping her arms around his waist and resting her face against his solid back.

"Oh yeah?" he said with a chuckle.

"Mhmm."

He turned around, but she continued to hold on to him, tilting back her head to gaze into his eyes. "Everything okay at work?" she asked.

"Yeah, why?"

"You seem off, tonight."

"Do I?"

"Yes." They'd spent enough time with each other and talking on the phone that she thought she knew his personality well.

He eased away, leaving her bereft of his touch. Her arms hung limply at her sides as he created distance between them by walking over to the island. Resting his back against it, he crossed his arms and looked at her.

"I want to ask you something," he said.

"Go ahead," she said, a clump of dread taking up residence in the pit of her stomach.

"We're having a birthday party for a friend of mine next week, and I want you to come with me."

She shook her head. "I can't."

"I knew you were going to say that, and yet..."

"I told you that my husband's family—"

"None of them will be at the party."

"How do you know that? You don't know who knows who in this city. Can we just leave things the way they are?"

"You're happy with one night a week and nothing more?"

"It's not one night a week. It's more like one night and one day a week. From the beginning, I've stayed with you on Saturdays."

Axel blew out a frustrated breath. "It's not good enough anymore."

"That's not what we agreed to."

"Yeah," he said bitterly, running a frustrated hand over his head.

"What do you want from me?"

"I want *you*. More of you." He thrust both hands at her to emphasize the point.

It was Naphressa's turn to cross her arms over her chest. "I'm not ready for that. It's only been a month. I still don't know if you're real."

"If I'm real? What the hell does that mean?"

His irritation at her sparked irritation *in* her. "You want to know what that means? I'll tell you. You told me once that you 'date a lot.'" She used air quotes. "Don't you think I would be a little foolish not to be cautious when I was married to a man who slept around, too? He cheated on me not only before we were married but while we were married."

"I'm not Byron," he said testily.

"No, you're not, but some of your actions are awfully similar to his. He did all the right things and said all the right things, like you. What really happened between you and your ex-fiancée? Was she the reason you bought this house—a family home in a family neighborhood, and she just walked away from you and this gorgeous place?"

"Yes, she chose this house, but like I told you, she moved on."

"Why? You were giving her everything she wanted."

"Not everything," he grated.

"What do you mean?"

He paused, thoughtfully rubbing his bearded jaw. "I loved Rose, but she and I would have never lasted, and I realize that now. In a way, she did us both a favor, but I didn't see it at the time. She would have never been completely happy because marrying me would have meant setting aside her dreams. She knew I wanted kids and a family and wasn't moving out of Georgia—not with my elderly parents living only a couple hours away in Augusta. I want to be close to them. She had no ties to Georgia and was focused and ambitious, and believe me,

I understand being focused and ambitious. I'm the same way, but I can achieve my goals in Atlanta. She couldn't."

"Why do you think she never said anything before you bought this place?"

"Knowing Rose, she probably thought it was the right path —getting married and settling down here. Then the job opportunity came up, and she couldn't lie to herself—or me—anymore." He shrugged.

"I'd be upset if I bought a house and decorated it for the person who bailed on me. Why aren't you bitter?"

"What makes you think I'm not?" Axel asked.

"You don't act like it. You seem rather well-adjusted."

He laughed shortly. "I wasn't for a long time. Matter of fact, I've been called..." He let the words trail off, as if he wasn't sure he should share that bit of information with her. "I've been called withdrawn and aloof. Then I ran into you, and now none of that matters."

Ever since she'd met him, he'd managed to make her feel like she was an exceptional woman, through his words, or by the way he looked at her or touched her. There had been a period of time when she felt that way with her husband, but he'd changed after, and his infidelities had poked holes in her confidence.

"I changed you?" she asked casually, to downplay her deep-seated desire to hear him say *Yes*.

"Yes, you did, and gave me a different perspective. I know you think I'm bullshitting when I tell you how much you mean to me, but I'm not. I was determined to find you, one way or the other."

"You weren't looking for me," Naphressa said, ears perked up to hear what she hoped was a rebuttal.

"Says who? If I'd had your *real name*, I probably would have found you before we ran into each other at my office," Axel said, giving her a pointed look.

Heat burned her cheeks. "Fine, yes, I gave you a fake name. But you probably only looked for me what...a day or two maybe? After that, you probably said, *Oh no, I can't find her, so I better stop looking.*"

Axel chuckled softly, shaking his head. "You really don't believe me, do you?"

"I learned the hard way that men will say and do whatever to get you, but their word is often worth less than nil."

By all accounts, her father had pursued her mother with tenacity, until she finally gave in. Byron had wined and dined her, seduced her with sweet words filled with declarations of love, and made her believe she'd rocked his world. In reality, she'd simply been a way to get his parents off his back. They'd wanted him to settle down, to be ready to take over their real estate empire. So he'd settled down, but after a time, she'd come to realize that she was living in a loveless marriage. The truth had been disheartening as well as painful.

Silence filled the kitchen as Axel continued to stare at her. She fought the urge to squirm, staring right back at him.

He broke the silence with a quiet voice. "I was planning a trip back to Belize to question every single employee at our resort. I even set up a meeting with a sketch artist to draw a picture of you that I could take with me to show around."

Stunned, Naphressa's mouth slowly fell open. "You're kidding."

Instead of responding, Axel picked up his phone from where it was charging on the counter. After a few clicks, he handed it to her. She looked at the screen and gasped.

"What's this?" she asked, though she knew exactly what she was looking at.

"What does it look like?"

"An American Airlines flight confirmation to Belize."

"Then that's what it is."

"You were really going back there?" she whispered.

"Believe me now?"

Naphressa swallowed the lump in her throat. "I guess I don't have much of a choice, do I?"

He cupped her face. "You don't have to come to the birthday party. I want you to meet my friends and spend time with me outside of this house, but you don't have to come. I'll leave early, call you when I'm on my way home, and we can get together afterward."

"I don't want you to leave your friends because of me."

"I want to," Axel said. "Look, I admit to being impatient, but you're right, it's only been a month, and it's clear Byron messed with your head in a major way. But don't doubt my feelings for you. They're real. They're intense. They keep me up at night. Take all the time you need to get used to me. I'm not going anywhere." He smiled. "You're stuck with my ass."

11

"Where are you?" Hazel asked.

"At the mall, looking for a gift for Taylor's birthday," Naphressa replied. She had a Bluetooth inserted into her ear while she lifted different articles of clothing, trying to decide which one to purchase for her nephew.

"I told you what he wanted."

"Yes, I know. I already bought the game, but I want to add to it. Maybe a nice jacket for church?"

"He wouldn't care, but I'd like that. In addition to feeding kids, clothing them is expensive, too. Consider yourself lucky."

"Am I lucky?" Naphressa mused.

"What do you mean?"

"I mean, I don't know...I've been thinking a lot lately, about marriage and kids." She fingered a display filled with ties. Specifically, marriage and kids with Axel. She suspected he'd be a great dad and husband.

"Okay. Huh. I thought you were through with the idea of getting married again, at least for a while. Where did that come from?"

"Been doing some thinking, that's all."

"Has this come about because of a certain corporate attorney who works for Abraham, MacKenzie & Wong?"

"*Maybe.*" Naphressa picked up an orange and blue tie and then set it back down.

"Okay, what's going on?"

"Hell if I know." Naphressa let out a heavy sigh. "I'm all mixed up, and I need to talk. I'm leaving here in a little bit. Let me finish my shopping and I'll stop by your house so we can talk."

"Yes, do that, because this conversation is different from ones we've had in the past. I'll be done cooking by the time you get here, so you can eat dinner with us."

"All right. See you when I get there."

Naphressa walked around the store a little longer, searching through the racks and tables for the perfect gift for her nephew. After a while, she found the cutest little tan jacket with a red and tan pocket square. She took it to the salesperson, and he helped her pick a shirt and tie to go with the jacket.

Satisfied with the purchases, she was about to leave the store when she passed by the men's section. Her footsteps slowed as she thought about Axel. He was such a nice dresser, she wondered if she could pick clothes for him that he'd like. Before their relationship fell apart, she used to like shopping for Byron. There was something satisfying about dressing her man in clothing and colors that looked good on him.

"Axel's not your man," she chided herself in a low voice.

Dismissing her silly idea, she continued striding toward the door, but then stopped. She could get him something, couldn't she? It wouldn't change the nature of their relationship. And after all, so far he'd been extremely good to her. Each time she came over to his house, he cooked dinner and breakfast the next morning. She was actually getting used to being catered to.

"I'll get him something small," she murmured.

She turned around and went back to the men's section. There were so many options, and she could envision Axel in each jacket or tie or casualwear. He was tall and clothes fit his body well. She knew that almost anything she purchased would look good on him.

Finally, she settled on a lavender shirt with a black and purple plaid tie, something he could wear to work. She bought the items and rushed out of the store before she changed her mind.

As Naphressa entered her sister's kitchen, her nephew Taylor came rushing at her legs. "Hi, Auntie Nessa!" he screamed.

"How's my big boy?" Naphressa bent down and gave him a tight squeeze.

"Good. Look." The six-year-old grinned up at her, showing off his missing front teeth.

"Oh, my goodness! You lost more teeth?"

"And the tooth fairy left me five dollars under my pillow." Taylor's eyes widened.

"Five dollars? The tooth fairy has really stepped her game up since I was a kid." Naphressa locked eyes with her sister, who was busy setting the table.

The sisters looked very much alike. Both had dusky-dark skin and Hazel was only half an inch taller, barely noticeable. But unlike Naphressa, she wore her raven hair straight.

Hazel shrugged. "The 'tooth fairy' overdid it and has created some lofty expectations in these children. I tried to tell the tooth fairy it was too much, but he didn't listen."

That meant Hazel and her husband, Darren, had disagreed about how much to give the kids for their teeth. Hazel didn't work, but she took care of the family budget, paid the bills, and managed the savings account. Her husband left everything to her but could be a bit extravagant with his spending habits. It was thanks to Hazel that they were able to maintain a fairly comfortable standard of living even though she hadn't worked full-time since a few years after they married.

"Well, I guess it's okay to splurge every now and again, isn't it?" Naphressa asked.

"It's fine, but when you're saving for a vacation for a family of five, being prudent is a lot better than being extravagant in most cases. Anyway, I didn't want to make a big deal out of it and dropped the topic. You need to change clothes?"

"Yes. Do you mind?"

"Check the second drawer in my dresser. I should have some clean T-shirts and sweatpants in there you can wear."

Naphressa went into the bedroom. She peeped at her niece sleeping in a bassinet near the bed, smiling at her plump cheeks and the way she breathed through her mouth. She then hung up the jacket and other items she'd bought for Taylor in the closet, careful to remove the tags.

She found a T-shirt and pair of orange sweats right where her sister said they'd be. Hazel was a size bigger, but the clothes were comfy and perfect for lounging around the house in. As she exited the bedroom, Darren and the other two boys arrived.

"We're back!" Darren called, heading toward the kitchen. He was about six four with a heavy voice.

"Is that Auntie Nessa's car outside?" she heard her oldest nephew ask.

"It sure is," she answered, coming into the kitchen.

The eight-year-old and three-year-old boys, who'd gone to the store with their father, let out a yell of surprise and barreled toward her with arms outstretched and big grins on their faces. After the greetings and hugs were over, they all sat around the dinner table. The boys ate chicken fingers and macaroni and cheese with a side of broccoli, while the adults had a similar meal, except with fried chicken.

Afterward, Naphressa helped Hazel clean up while Darren took the boys into the den. When they finished in the kitchen, Naphressa sat down on the couch and her sister plopped down beside her.

"You look tired," Naphressa said.

"I am, a little. But I'm going to savor this moment while Darren has the boys occupied and you and I get to talk."

At thirty-five years old, Hazel was three years older than Naphressa. They had always been close, but each had taken different paths in life. Hazel was married to her high school sweetheart. She and Darren had been together off and on since their junior year in high school. For almost 10 years, they'd been in and out of each other's life, until Hazel grew tired of the back-and-forth and told him she needed a clean break and was moving away.

Darren wasn't having it. He finally came to his senses. Not wanting to lose her, he proposed within a matter of days, and within a year they were married. As far as Naphressa knew, Hazel had never regretted the decision to stay with Darren, nor the decision to give up her career in communications, no matter how much she complained about her kids and her life-style. Naphressa knew she was exactly where she wanted to be.

On the other hand, Naphressa had been slow to figure out what she wanted to do, skipped college and went straight into the workforce. She held a multitude of different jobs—working as an administrative assistant, working in restaurants, and at one point doing janitorial work at night while she took real estate sales classes during the day. In the end, she finally settled on property management and met the man who she thought would be her lifelong partner. She couldn't have been more wrong.

She'd wanted the type of love her sister had with Darren, but that was not to be.

No fairytale for her. Only harsh reality.

Resting an elbow on the back of the sofa, Hazel crossed one leg over the other and gave Naphressa her undivided attention. "So what's going on with you and Axel? And by the way, aren't you usually with him on a Friday night?"

"Usually." She hadn't told her sister the true nature of their relationship, but Hazel knew that Friday nights was their night to spend time together. "But tonight he's at a birthday party for one of his friends."

"And you didn't go with him?" Hazel frowned.

"He asked if I wanted to go, but I declined," Naphressa replied, her sister's reaction making her feel guilty.

"Why?"

"Because it would be too...intimate? I mean, once you a meet a man's friends, that changes everything, doesn't it?"

"It could. How did he react when you turned him down?"

"He wasn't happy but he said he'd be patient. He's leaving the party early, and he'll give me a call when he does so we can meet at his house."

"Help me to understand what's going on here. You said over the phone that you're starting to think about marriage and kids. If you really like this guy, why are you pulling back from him?"

"That's the million-dollar question. Part of it is because...I guess I'm scared." That was hard to admit openly, even to her sister, her best friend.

"Of being hurt again?"

"Yes." She cast her eyes downward.

"Based on everything you've told me, he sounds like a really good person. Has he given you any reason to doubt his sincerity?"

"None, but in a lot of ways he reminds me of Byron, which makes me suspicious."

"How is he like Byron?"

"For one, he's into me. I mean, really into me, the way Byron was. He's also an only child, handsome, and a sweet talker."

Hazel twisted her pouted lips to one side. "I get what you're saying, *but…*"

"I know, I know, I shouldn't judge him by my past experience with Byron, but I can't help it. He constantly reminds me of him."

"Do you think he's being fake? If you have reservations, you should go with your gut."

Naphressa temporarily covered her face and let out a groan. "I don't know! I'm worried that maybe I'm not a very good judge of character and could be falling for the same trick again. I don't want to end up like…you know."

Sympathy filled Hazel's eyes. "Yeah, I know."

Their mother.

Their father had been a jerk who ranted at their mother often and harshly. He never hit her, that Naphressa knew of, but he battered her self-esteem with verbal blows. The sisters' bond was irrevocable because of what they'd seen as children, but their past affected them in different ways. Hazel escaped to college and never went back home. Neither did Naphressa after she graduated high school, but she wandered aimlessly through life for a while, trying to figure out what she wanted to do.

Looking at past photos, it was clear their father's constant belittling and verbal barbs had made their mother shrink from the outgoing young woman she'd been when they met, to a closed-off adult who looked ten years older than she really was when she passed in her early fifties. Estranged from his daughters, their father passed only months later, as if he couldn't stand to be alone with no one to pick on anymore.

"I understand why you would have reservations, but I think you're going to hurt herself in the long run. Why don't you do this—enjoy yourself. Don't overthink your relationship with Axel. And the next time he invites you to an activity planned with friends, maybe say yes and see how it goes?"

"Easier said than done. There aren't a lot of Darrens out there." Darren was the opposite of their father, and Naphressa had thought she'd found someone like him in Byron. She couldn't believe how wrong she'd been.

"True. I lucked out." Hazel flashed a grin. "But you know I'm right. You can't let fear run your life forever."

"You're right. I know I'm doing it, but I can't stop."

Hazel patted her knee. "It's only been a year since Byron passed away. Give yourself time, but don't limit yourself, either. If Axel is as great as you say, he'll continue to prove himself worthy of your time."

12

S he took him up on his offer to paint at his house.

After lunch on Saturday, Naphressa set up her easel and paints and went to work. He also invited her to spend the evening with him, so for the first time they were going to spend the entirety of Saturday and Saturday night together. She couldn't deny being a little excited when she accepted his offer.

The sunlight coming in through the windows was magnificent, and she chose to paint the photos she'd taken of the Brixton building the other day. Axel worked on his laptop at the breakfast table instead of in his office, for which she was glad, because even though they weren't talking to each other, she enjoyed having his presence thereby.

They already had a weekly routine, which she'd grown accustomed to. So much for her determination to keep their relationship purely sexual. Her so-called resolve was already crumbling.

She only wished she could paint portraits. If she could, she would paint him as she saw him in this moment, with his attention focused on the screen in front of him. Every now and again he frowned and then rubbed his bearded chin. Did he have any idea how sexy he looked doing that?

Her ringing phone pulled her from her trance. "Hey, sis, what's up?" she said.

"I need a *huge* favor. The babysitter canceled on us, and Darren got us tickets to see Sinbad at the Cobb Center. I hate to ask last minute, but do you mind watching the kids for us tonight?"

"Of course not." There went the prospect of spending the evening with Axel, gone as quickly as it had come. "I have plans tonight, but I can postpone them."

He looked up at her then, his eyes questioning.

"You sure?" Hazel asked, sounding hesitant.

"Absolutely."

"I knew having a little sister would come in handy one day."

"Ha, ha. Just tell me what time you need me to be at your house, and make it fast before I change my mind."

Hazel laughed, sounding a lot more relieved than she did when she initially called. "Can you be here by five? You'll need to order dinner for the kids later. A pizza or something should be fine. You know where I keep the coupons in the kitchen drawer, and I went to the store earlier today, so there're also plenty of snacks in the pantry. Please don't eat them all and save some for the boys."

"I'm starting to rethink my decision to help you."

"Don't! I'll stop. Five, okay? Don't forget."

"I'll see you then." Naphressa hung up and walked over to where Axel was still looking at her at the kitchen table.

"Sounds like we'll have to postpone our plans tonight," he said, sitting back in the chair.

She nodded. "I'm really sorry, but Hazel and Darren need me. Their babysitter canceled and they have plans tonight. Maybe you and I could spend time together tomorrow night?"

"Yeah. Maybe tomorrow night."

He looked disappointed, and she hated to be the one to change their plans, but it couldn't be avoided. "At least we have the rest of the afternoon together, until five."

"Perfect," he said in an emotionless voice. She couldn't read his expression

"Okay, great. We'll plan to be together tomorrow or another day. I'm going to see how much of this painting I can get done before I leave."

He didn't say another word and went back to work, and she walked back over to the easel. She glanced at him. He'd seemed oddly detached by the cancelation.

Then she had a thought, something so completely unexpected that she wasn't sure she should voice it. How many times had he shown her how important she was to him? He'd invited her to hang out with him and his friends and made sure she felt welcomed every time she set foot in his house.

"Hey, I have an idea," she said.

He looked up from the computer. "Yeah?"

"Why don't you come with me?"

His eyebrows shot toward the ceiling. "To your sister's house?"

"Yes. You and I can still spend time together, and I'll get to see if you're any good with kids."

A sexy smile spread across his lips. "Oh, kids love me."

"Is that right?"

"I've never lied to you yet."

"No, you haven't, have you?" The moment stretched between them. "So you'll come?"

"Yes, I'd like to."

"And then I'll introduce you to my sister."

"I'd really like that," he said, with heartfelt appreciation.

It dawned on her that he'd been waiting for her to make the suggestion. To invite him into her world the way he'd invited her into his.

"Then it's a date."

"A date with three little boys and a little girl. Sounds like the perfect evening." His smile was all she needed to see to know that he was all in.

"We'll see how perfect you think the evening is at the end of the night."

"Wait a minute..."

She laughed and then turned her attention back to the easel.

"Am I getting myself into a situation I should be concerned about?"

"Don't worry your handsome little head about a thing. You're about to have an evening that you won't forget."

She didn't say another word, but she laughed internally as he continued to watch her for a few seconds longer, probably trying to determine whether or not she was kidding.

But she was *not* kidding.

"NICE TO FINALLY MEET YOU," Hazel said, extending her hand to Axel. Her hands were cool and soft, and she and Naphressa looked very much alike, making it obvious they were sisters. "I'm sorry we have to rush out. Maybe another day we can spend time getting to know each other. Dinner or some other event...?" She glanced at her sister, as if to make sure the invitation was acceptable.

"I think that would be a great idea, don't you?" Naphressa asked him.

"I definitely like it," Axel said.

Darren, standing behind his wife, placed a hand on her shoulder. "It was nice meeting you, Axel. Baby, we better get going because you know it's going to take a while for us to get up there, and then we have to find parking in that place. We better head out so we're not rushing."

"He's right. See you guys later." Hazel waved and the two of them left.

The door closed and Naphressa swung to face him. "Time for you to meet the boys," she said ominously, taking his hand.

The fact that he was here, and that she casually took his hand, was a big deal. Their relationship had blossomed over time, and she was much more comfortable with him.

She led him into the den, where the boys were lounging on the floor playing with a train set and toy trucks. Other toys were scattered around the room and on top of the bean bag chairs and older-looking sofas.

Before she could begin the introductions, one of the boys, who was missing two front teeth, asked, "Auntie Nessa, who's your friend?"

"Boys, this is Axel. Axel, these are my nephews. Taylor is the one who asked the question. He's six and the most talkative."

"I am not!" the little boy denied hotly.

"See?" she told him.

Axel laughed. "Nice to meet you, Taylor."

"That's Bradley, the youngest boy at three, and that's Darren Junior, the oldest. He's eight. The baby's asleep in Hazel and Darren's room."

"Nice to meet you, boys. I guess we'll be hanging out a little bit tonight."

"Do you know how to fight?" Taylor asked, his eyes hopeful.

"Fight?" Axel asked, glancing at Naphressa. He hadn't expected *that* question.

"They like to sword-fight and wrestle," Naphressa explained. "Something they and their dad do on a regular basis. I can, however, kick their butts anywhere and any time that I choose." She mean-mugged Taylor.

"No, you can't," Taylor insisted, his eyes lighting up with excitement.

Little Bradley came to stand beside his brother. "We're kicking *your* butt, Auntie!" he declared in a little squeaky voice.

"Guess we'll see about that," Naphressa said.

She grabbed the smallest one and flung him over her shoulder.

"Put me down!" he hollered, kicking his feet and giggling at the same time.

"Come on, who's next?" she said.

She started running around the den, and the other boys chased her while she kept a giggling Bradley looped over one shoulder. Axel stood back, wondering if he should jump in, when a pillow hit him upside the head. Stunned, he turned to face Junior, who held a colorful foam sword in his hand. There was apparently no way to simply be a spectator.

"On guard!" Junior said, hopping into position and baring his teeth like fangs.

Axel grabbed another sword and tossed it from hand to hand. "You don't want none of this," he warned. He bared his teeth, too, and jumped into the fray.

Before long, the den was filled with screaming boys and adults as they chased each other around, sword fighting and tossing pillows—which the boys had dubbed grenades—at each other.

At one point, Naphressa was buried under a pile of little legs and hands, but Axel came to her rescue and scooped up Taylor and Bradley, while she playfully placed a squealing Junior in a headlock.

Axel lifted Bradley over his head and fake-slammed him onto one of the sofas. The boy rolled off, giggling, and jumped up at Axel with his arms outstretched.

"Again!" he screamed.

Over and over again, he alternated between slamming

Bradley, throwing grenades at Taylor, and sword-fighting with Junior. At some point, Junior declared that he and his brothers were The Three Musketeers, and Naphressa and Axel were the married king and queen who wanted to stop their adventures. Every few minutes, Axel caught Naphressa's eye, and she was grinning from ear to ear.

They had fun for a long time, until Taylor went racing into his parents' bedroom and woke up his little sister. That brought the playing to a screeching halt. After a quick scolding by Naphressa, she rocked little Regina back to sleep while the boys waited impatiently for the games to resume.

Axel watched her from his position on the floor with a sulking Taylor seated on his lap. She was a natural, sitting there with her niece swaying in her arms, whispering quietly until the baby's eyes started to droop.

He could absolutely see Naphressa as a mother, and could well imagine the pain she experienced when her husband told her he didn't want kids. It was so obvious that she loved children, and given what she had told him about the dysfunction in her upbringing, he imagined she'd be very conscientious about being a good parent. He wanted to be the one to give her those kids. He wanted to be the one to give her everything her heart desired, and more.

He thought of the emptiness of his life before her—including all of the emotionless sex that had satisfied his physical being but did little to gratify the inner part of him that required a deeper connection. Those women had been a way for him to fill the time, but he wanted a wife and family. He longed for someone to share his dreams with. He longed for a woman to come home to, to spoil, and to be the type of man who made her acknowledge that no one else would do. Their time together confirmed what he'd assumed in Belize. Naphressa was that woman.

She left the room with the sleeping baby in her arms. When

she returned, she spoke in a quiet voice. "Okay, I got Regina back to sleep. We're going to have to keep it down and stay out of Mommy and Daddy's room, okay?"

The boys nodded their understanding.

"Okay," Taylor said glumly.

"Can we still fight?" Bradley asked, his eyes round and anxious.

"Yes, we can," Naphressa answered.

"In that case..." Axel jumped to his feet and snatched one of the foam swords from the floor. "On guard!" He pressed the tip into Junior's chest.

"You're a dead man, sir!" Junior declared.

"No, you, sir!"

Their fight began again, with The Three Musketeers battling for their lives against the cruel king and queen.

Axel didn't know when the last time was that he'd ever had so much fun.

13

"I can't believe you eat this crap," Axel muttered, wrinkling his nose at the large pineapple and ham pizza he set on the table. They'd ordered two pizzas. The other was pepperoni. "And you feed it to your nephews. Does your sister know the kind of abuse you inflict on them when she's not around?"

The boys were in the den watching the movie *Abominable*.

Naphressa rolled her eyes at him. "Don't give me a hard time because you stick to the same-old, same-old pepperoni and cheese."

"Because it tastes good and pepperoni is the most popular pizza topping. Ham and pineapple, however, is an abomination."

"Says you."

"Says the majority of self-respecting pizza eaters."

"Here's the thing. I don't care what the majority of self-respecting pizza eaters think." She stuck out her tongue.

Axel glanced over his shoulder to make sure the kids remained occupied. Then he cornered Naphressa against the kitchen counter.

"Pepperoni is way better than that crap. Let me hear you say it."

"So you want me to lie, counselor?" she asked.

"I'd prefer that you didn't. Do you swear to tell the truth, the whole truth, and nothing but the truth, so help you God?"

"I do."

Those deep, dark eyes smiled up at him, and he had that familiar tension in his stomach that let him know how important she'd become in his life. He was enjoying himself immensely, even though they weren't alone and had spent the evening playing with three rambunctious little boys.

"I'm really glad I came tonight," Axel said.

"I'm glad you came, too, and I have something to tell you." She spoke slowly and quietly, and he sensed what she was about to say would be very important.

"What do you have to tell me?"

Swallowing, she hooked a finger in the waistband of his jeans. "That I've never felt this way before. That I'm enjoying myself, and looking at you with my nephews makes me think that you really are a good guy. The kind of guy that I've been looking for. And..."

"And...?" He anxiously waited for her to add to the sentence.

"I want us to learn more about each other and get closer, outside of your house. I would love to meet your friends."

"You mean that?" He wondered if she could hear how fast his heart was beating.

"I mean it," Naphressa said quietly.

He bent his head and kissed her lips, teasing them open with his tongue. "You're not afraid anymore?"

"I trust you more than I'm afraid."

He recognized the honor she'd bestowed on him by giving him her trust. "I won't let you down. I promise."

"You better not." She bunched the front of his shirt into her fist and pulled him closer for another kiss. This one was lip-smackingly deep and made his head spin.

After they came up for air, he muttered against her mouth, "You better stop before we get out of control."

"You mean, because you can't resist me?" she teased, nipping his bottom lip with her teeth.

"Oh, so it's like that?"

She laughed against his mouth, her warm breath tapping against his lips. Her laughter was as refreshing as opening the windows and letting in air on a balmy day. Their intimate moment was not meant to last, however.

"*Yuck.* Stop kissing." Bradley's voice dripped with disgust. "Why are grown-ups always kissing?"

No doubt he'd seen his parents in a lip lock or two.

Axel swept the little boy into his arms, enjoying his squeals of joy. "One of these days, my man, you'll understand."

Junior came out of the den. "I'm hungry. Can we eat now?" He eyed the pizzas on the table.

"Yes, you can. I need the three of you to go wash your hands right now. Chop, chop," Naphressa said, clapping her hands.

Axel placed Bradley back on his feet, and he scurried after his older brothers.

Naphressa rose up on her toes and kissed him on the lips, cradling his head between her hands.

"Didn't you hear, that was yucky," Axel said.

"I heard, but I couldn't help myself."

He lowered his lips to hers one more time, because he couldn't help himself, either.

Then he and Naphressa set about getting plates and drinks together for their pizza dinner.

"Hey."

That was her sister's voice, and her sister's hand gently shaking her shoulder.

Naphressa's eyes fluttered open.

She smothered a yawn with the back of her hand. "You're back," she whispered.

"Looks like you guys had a great time," Hazel said softly. Darren stood beside her, shaking his head, a little smile on his face.

The TV was about halfway through another movie, *Coco*. Naphressa had fallen asleep on one end of the sofa with Regina in her arms. She'd had to feed the baby earlier when she had woken up again. Axel was on the opposite end of the sofa, his head resting against its back. Taylor sat on his lap, with a perfect circle of drool wetting Axel's shirt next to the boy's mouth. Junior was fast asleep on the floor with his head cushioned on a bunched up throw, while Bradley lay sprawled on the second sofa by himself.

"We did."

"And he didn't run off. That's a good sign," Hazel said.

"I've had a lot of good signs with him," Naphressa said, glancing at Axel.

She then met her sister's eyes, and an understanding passed between them.

"I'll put Regina to bed," Naphressa said.

"And I'll get Bradley. Baby, would you get Taylor?" Hazel said, turning to her husband.

The three of them worked in silence. When Taylor was lifted from his arms, Axel woke up and stretched and acknowledged Hazel and Darren with a head nod. They exited with the kids in their arms.

Naphressa went back into the den and saw Darren shaking Taylor awake. "Say good night," he told his son.

"'Night," Junior mumbled. He paused at the door and cast a

look in Axel's direction. "Are you gonna come back and fight with us again?"

Axel opened his mouth but seemed unsure how to answer the question. Naphressa was amused to see him speechless for once.

"Yes, he will," she answered on his behalf.

"Cool," Junior said.

"Good night," Darren said, following his son from the room.

Hazel escorted Naphressa and Axel to the front door.

"How was the show?" Naphressa asked.

"Excellent, as always. He's still funny as heck."

"Glad you had a good time. There's a couple pieces of pizza left in a box in the fridge."

"It's not that nasty pineapple and ham, is it?" Hazel wrinkled her nose.

"Don't start. The boys like it. You don't have to eat it."

"I'm so glad I'm not alone," Axel murmured beside her.

Naphressa elbowed him in the torso and he groaned.

"Can I give you a hug? I've been trying to convert her to normal toppings for years." Hazel opened her arms.

"Absolutely." They hugged and Naphressa rolled her eyes.

"Enough of that, please. We gotta go. Good night."

"Good night." Hazel gave Naphressa a quick squeeze and then closed the door.

They walked down the steps of the house and climbed into Axel's car.

On the drive over, he said, "You might as well stay the night at my place. It's late."

"I guess that would make sense." From the passenger seat, she watched his profile in the dark. The way he drove was sexy, with one muscular arm casually looped over the wheel, his body relaxed.

"I need to get something from my car when we get back to your place."

"Okay," he said.

In the garage at his house, Naphressa opened the trunk of her car and took out the bag with the shirt and tie she'd purchased for him. She trailed him up the stairs to his bedroom, where a king bed sat in the middle of one wall.

Axel stripped off his shirt and kicked his shoes into the closet. "What is that?" he asked, nodding toward the bag. "A change of clothes?"

"Actually, something I bought for you."

He sank onto the bed and frowned at her. "For me? Did I miss an anniversary or something?"

"No, I bought it just because."

"Oh yeah?"

Suddenly feeling shy, Naphressa nodded. "Yes."

She handed over the bag. He opened it and pulled out the lavender shirt and tie.

"I saw it and thought of you, but if you don't like this combination, I can take them both back."

His eyes met hers, but there was no cockiness or arrogance evident in his face. Only a deep sense of appreciation. "I like them. A lot. Thank you."

"You're welcome."

Running his fingers over the front of the shirt, Axel asked, "When did you get this?"

"A while back," she said dismissively.

"How far back?"

"A few weeks ago."

"What made you give it to me now?"

She swallowed, the truth staring her in her face. "Just felt right."

"I know all about that," Axel said in a solemn tone. He set aside the shirt and pulled her between his knees. "Is this the part where I give you sex as a thank you?"

Naphressa laughed, tossing back her head, happy to break

the solemnness of the last few moments. "Are you trying to say that's what women do, or is it what men expect?"

"Don't put words in my mouth."

"Then answer the question, counselor."

"I plead the fifth."

"Spoken like a true attorney." She gazed down into his upturned face and looped her arms around his neck. Her heart was full. Her heart was happy. Axel made her happy. "I'll take the sex now, please."

"Coming right up, but, before we get started, I want to throw out an idea to you. Let's go away together, just the two of us. Do you have plans Memorial Day weekend? We could drive down to south Georgia or better yet, to Hilton Head. My parents own a condo on the beach there, which they rarely use. What do you think?"

"I think it's a great idea, and I'd love to go."

He blessed her with one of his sexy smiles. "Perfect."

Naphressa cleared her throat loudly and unsnapped his jeans. "Now, about that sex…"

"I'm only having sex with you because I want to, not because I feel obligated," Axel said, palming her butt.

Her body awakened to his touch, and she dropped a kiss to his cheek. "There's no better reason to do anything in this world."

14

"Hey, Randy!"

Naphressa greeted the security guard at the front desk as she came in from lunch. He was usually here when she returned and took his lunch when the other guard came back. A couple of years ago, he'd jumped her battery in the parking lot after hours one night, and ever since then they'd been friends.

"Hi, Naphressa. Guess what?" A grin of utter joy spread across his baby face as he leaned an elbow on the high desk. "We found a house, and it's under contract."

Naphressa squealed her delight and desperately wanted to grab him in a hug, but that would be way too inappropriate. "Oh my goodness! Congratulations, future homeowner!"

She couldn't have been happier if she herself had found the perfect home. Randy was under thirty but newly married with a baby on the way. They talked a while back about his desire to purchase a home, but he'd run into a problem. He didn't have bad credit, he just didn't have *any* credit. He and his wife had been very careful not to accrue any debt, but that wasn't good when one was looking to purchase a home with a mortgage.

Though she dealt exclusively with commercial real estate nowadays, Naphressa's brief stint in real estate sales had given her a network of contacts she could reach out to, and she'd connected him with a mortgage broker who was able to work with his situation.

"When do you close?"

"End of May." He held up crossed fingers on both hands.

"I can't wait. I'm going to get you the best housewarming gift."

"I should get you a gift for walking me through the process. If it weren't for you, we wouldn't be so close to buying our own home."

"You'd have found a way, but I'm glad I could help. I'm writing down the closing date so I can get you a little something, but please send me pictures of your new place, okay?"

"Definitely."

No sooner had the words left his mouth than a shadow came over Randy's face. His smile faltered as he looked past her.

"Good afternoon, Mr. Hayes," he said, way more serious now.

Naphressa snapped to attention. There was something about Victor Hayes that dimmed the light in every room he entered.

"Randy," the older man said, in a cultured voice.

That's how he greeted everyone. Never with a good morning or a good day. He simply called them by their first name.

Victor Hayes was tall, lean, and broad shouldered. He was baldheaded, with deep lines at his mouth and eyes—odd for a man who never smiled. Those lines had deepened since Byron passed. He'd adored his son. Naphressa's thumb touched the ring on her finger, which in light of her relationship with Axel felt more like a noose than ever before.

Randy sat down and his attention was suddenly taken up by the computer screen, which meant the conversation was over. Victor owned the building, so essentially he was Randy's boss. He knew better than to be seen fraternizing with other employees, because Victor didn't approve of the guards getting too friendly, which could affect their ability to do their job well.

Naphressa followed Victor to the elevator. As they waited outside the doors, she remembered that Axel had invited her on a mini vacation, and she wanted to put in a request for the time off. No time like the present to bring up the topic.

The elevator doors opened, and she stepped into the cabin and stood on the opposite end, away from Victor.

"Did you have a nice lunch?" she asked to warm him up to the conversation.

"It was fine," he replied in a bored voice. Naphressa had never gotten used to his disinterested tone.

She cleared her throat. "I'll submit a formal request, but I was wondering offhand if you have any objection to me taking a long weekend around the end of May. A friend has a condo in Hilton Head and invited me to spend a few days there." That was probably more information than he needed, but being around him always made her nervous.

"A friend?"

There was no way he could know about her relationship with Axel, yet his question suggested he knew she was lying.

"Yes." This time she did not provide any additional information.

"I don't see any reason why not. Nothing's coming up that I can think of that would require you to remain in the city around that time."

"Great. I'll be sure to put in a request."

The doors opened and she rushed from the suffocating interior.

"Naphressa."

The hairs on the back of her neck stood up. Turning slowly, she faced Victor, unease gripping her insides. She'd never been completely at ease around him. He was always so aloof and seemed to judge her with his eyes. She hadn't always been this uncomfortable. The discomfort increased after Byron's death. A shift had taken place in her relationship with Victor, and she had begun to feel the weight of being tolerated. As if she didn't belong—not just in their family, but in the company. The ring on her finger had served as a sort of buffer to ensure that she stayed within Victor's good graces, but she now regretted that she'd worn it to appease him.

"You know we appreciate all the hard work you do here. You're an asset. Byron did well marrying you, and I wish he was alive to see how much further you've come. The Brixton deal is quite an accomplishment, and I don't know if I've told you before, but I appreciate you bringing it to our attention and all the hard work you've put in. I'm sure Byron is looking down and smiling from his position on high."

He looked at her expectantly, and she realized with a start that he was waiting for her to agree.

"Yes, I'm sure he is."

He nodded, acknowledging she'd said the right words. For a split second, his gaze landed on her left hand, and then there was a smile—if one could call the minuscule upward tilting of both corners of his mouth, a smile—and then he went down the hallway.

Naphressa hurried to her office, glad Loretta was not at her desk so she wouldn't be forced to indulge in idle chitchat. She closed the door and leaned back against it with relief. Only a couple more months, and the Brixton deal would be finalized, the Brixton employees would have job security, and then she'd leave. She couldn't stay any longer under the weight of the Hayes family thumb.

AXEL AND BRAXTON exited the café. They'd met for lunch near his office because Braxton was a network specialist and had a client on his side of town today. They strolled down the sidewalk to the office building where Axel worked and Braxton had left his car.

"So when are you headed to Hilton Head?" Braxton asked.

Axel had told him about the trip he had planned for him and Naphressa.

"Memorial Day weekend."

"You're cheesing so hard. You're really looking forward to it."

"Like I told you guys from the beginning, she's the one."

"She still wearing the ring?" Braxton asked.

"Unfortunately. Man, I hate it, but she doesn't wear it around me."

"She should leave that company," Braxton said.

"She knows she needs to but wants to close the Brixton deal first, which I understand. She doesn't want to walk away from the biggest accomplishment of her career. The buyout will be finalized soon and then she'll leave. She's already started quietly putting out feelers for other project management positions."

"You ever worry that you've found another Rose? Someone whose career is more important than your relationship?"

Axel thought for a minute and answered honestly. "I had doubts in the beginning, wondering if I'd stumbled into the same kind of relationship, one that would leave me disappointed in the end."

"And?"

"Naphressa's different, and I believe we want the same kind of relationship. I'm going to marry that woman."

Braxton's eyebrows lifted higher. "You're not playing around."

"Hell, I'm trying to be like you, big man."

His friend laughed. "A worthy goal, my brother, but I feel you. Londyn hits me the same way."

They stopped at the crosswalk and hurried across the street when the light changed.

"You remember when Dani called us out back in February, told us why she thought we'd never get married?" Axel asked.

"Sure do. I didn't appreciate it at the time, but her assessment of us was spot on."

"No doubt, but you know what I was thinking?" Axel came to a stop a few cars over from Braxton's Acura. "Dani doesn't have a man. She needs to examine herself and figure out why the hell *she's* not married."

"You're right, but can you really see Dani doing any type of self-reflection about why she has advice for everyone else but remains single?"

"Nah, I can't see it."

They both had a good laugh and then parted ways.

15

"What's all this?" Axel looked at the luggage Naphressa had stacked at the door, which included a large orange suitcase and the matching carry-on and shoulder bag.

"These are my bags for the trip," she replied.

"Baby, we'll be gone for four days, not four weeks. One small suitcase should be enough."

"*Should* be, but I wasn't sure what I wanted to wear, so I packed a variety of clothes to change into. We're not going on a plane, so I can be more flexible. And this bag"—she placed the smaller one over her shoulder and patted it—"is filled with snacks and has an insulated compartment, so I've got soda and water in here for us, too."

"You and your snacks."

"You're going to be glad I have these snacks. Mark my word."

"It's a four-hour drive," Axel stated.

"It could be longer because of the holiday and the number of cars on the road. We might get thirsty and want something to eat." She pasted a smile on her face, but he saw steely resolve in her eyes. She wasn't budging.

She was right about the possibility of the drive taking longer, but that didn't mean he agreed with the extra bags. With a heavy sigh, he picked up the suitcases and walked to the SUV he'd rented, a roomy Buick Enclave in metallic blue sitting on the park pad outside her townhouse.

After locking the front door, Naphressa followed behind him, set the bag on the back seat, and climbed into the passenger side of the vehicle. Axel placed her luggage in the back with his and then joined her inside.

"We're ready?" he asked, closing the door.

"Yes."

He turned to her. "You already used the bathroom?"

"*Yes*," Naphressa answered, sounding annoyed.

"Stove, iron, everything turned off?"

She rolled her eyes. "Yes."

"Because once we're on the highway, I'm not turning this car around."

Naphressa burst out laughing. "Would you just go!"

She had the prettiest smile. She wasn't wearing makeup, and her hair was pulled back in a bun, showing off small gold earrings in the shape of roses. Her attire consisted of a white T-shirt with the words Laugh Often printed in gold letters across her chest, a pair of cut-off denim shorts that showed off her toned legs, and gold sandals.

"Let me get a kiss first." Axel leaned across the console and gave her a peck on the lips.

Before long, they were on the highway going south with Michael Jackson's *Thriller* album bumping through the speakers on a low volume.

As predicted, traffic slowed on the highway, and the bottle-neck meant they'd arrive past their noon deadline. Three hours into the journey, Axel started getting a little hungry but didn't want to pull over.

"What kind of snacks do you have back there?" he asked.

"Oh, so now you—"

He placed a long finger over her lips. "Not another word unless you're telling me what's in that bag," he warned.

With a self-righteous giggle, Naphressa reached for the bag in the back seat and pulled out two chilled cans of Coke, pretzels, and a bag of chips. She popped open one of the cans before handing it to him.

They ate the snacks and drank the sodas while they chatted on the way. Finally, almost six hours after they'd pulled away from her townhouse, they arrived at the condo complex in Hilton Head. Axel drove through the gate and parked in the numbered spot in front of the five-story building.

"We're here," he announced.

They climbed out of the vehicle and stretched, then he took his suitcase and her larger one, while she dragged her rolling carry-on and had the smaller bag with the left-over snacks on her shoulder.

"How long have your parents owned this place?" Naphressa asked as they walked down the hallway to the unit.

"They bought it when I was in high school. My father bought it for my mother, for their twentieth anniversary." He opened the door and stepped back.

"Nice gift," Naphressa said, preceding him into the condo.

"It's also a nice investment for them. A property manager maintains it and rents to tourists."

"This is cute," Naphressa said, scanning the interior.

Containing two bedrooms and two baths, the unit was simply furnished. The white kitchen opened into the living room/dining room combo, where a dining table seated six and a chair, loveseat, and armchair were covered in white and blue nautical fabric—paying homage to the seaside location.

After Axel deposited the bags in the master bedroom, he found Naphressa outside, resting her elbows on the balcony railing. The balcony overlooked the large swimming pool and the beach a mere three-minute walk away. Families, couples, and solo travelers with their large umbrellas and colorful beach towels dotted the landscape as the glittering blue water lapped at the shore.

Axel stepped between the two reclined beach chairs to stand next to Naphressa.

"When was the last time you came here?" she asked.

"I haven't been in a few years. I used to come at least once a year."

"Why don't you come more often? It's only a short drive away."

"I don't know. I didn't have any reason to come."

He hadn't thought much about why, but he suddenly realized, like a lot of the other aspects in his life, he lost interest after his engagement ended. Except for the times he hung out with Cole and Braxton, and the occasional hook up with a woman, his life revolved around work and home. The trip to Belize had been highly unusual, but it had certainly provided the greatest return because he'd met her.

"Hopefully that'll change in the future," he added meaningfully.

"I'd be willing to accompany you again—you know, to keep you company. If you like."

"I would like that." He took Naphressa's hand and pulled her against his side, kissing her temple as they watched the vacationers frolicking in the surf and tanning under the warm sun.

After a few minutes, he asked, "You want to go down to the beach today?"

"I do, but I need something of substance to eat first. I've had nothing but chips and pretzels since breakfast this morning. I'm hungry."

"Me, too. Food first, then we go to the beach."

NAPHRESSA WORE a white coverup that loosely draped over her body with large sleeves and a short hem. The low neckline showed off the red and white bikini top she wore with a red bottom.

Axel wore gray and blue swim trunks that came almost to the knees. He flung a towel over his shoulder, and she was a little perturbed by the spurt of possessiveness she experienced when she thought of the women who'd have the pleasure of ogling his bare chest and muscular legs.

Per Axel's request, the property manager had stocked the refrigerator with groceries, and he removed several bottles of water from the fridge and tucked them into the small, soft-sided cooler he found in one of the kitchen cabinets. Naphressa inserted a bag of caramel popcorn into her beach bag with additional towels and tossed it over her shoulder.

The condo office provided them with chairs and an umbrella. After Axel signed them out, they donned sunglasses and left for the beach.

Seated in what she considered the perfect spot, Naphressa reclined the chair and inhaled the salty scent of the water in the air while she listened to the music of the ocean waves rolling in.

After a while, she heard Axel ask, "Ready to go in?"

"Ready."

Standing, she lifted off her cover-up and yelled, "Race you!"

She dashed across the sand but was no match for Axel's speed.

"Gotcha!" he said, sweeping her off her feet.

She let out a scream of laughter, trapped as he trudged toward the water with her wriggling in his arms.

"Put me down!" she demanded.

A few people turned in their direction, but for the most part the other beachgoers were preoccupied with their own activities. Axel crashed into the waves and cool water spattered over their sun-warmed skin. He dropped her unceremoniously into the ocean. Salt water covered her head, temporarily blocking out the sounds of screaming and playing around them and burning her eyes. She rebounded by bouncing onto her feet.

"Hope you learned a valuable lesson," Axel said.

She shoved her wet hair out of her face.

His laughter was infectious, his smile the kind that made knees week and hearts race. He looked like a sea god, with water dripping from his dark brown skin and sparkling like diamonds in his hair and beard.

"You make me sick." Naphressa pouted and turned her back on him.

"What did you say?" His arms rounded her waist and he pulled her against him.

She let out a squeal as they tussled in the water, but she was no match for him. He overpowered her and stole kisses from her lips while caressing her legs beneath the water's surface. That's how they spent much of the afternoon—wrestling in the water, chasing each other, and swim racing. He beat her soundly each time because of his height advantage and bigger muscles.

She was reminded that they'd spent their time in Belize in a similar fashion.

Axel eventually left the water, but Naphressa didn't want to leave. She remained for a few minutes longer, letting the sun beat down on her skin while she floated on her back. This was a lovely escape—one that she didn't know she'd needed. If today was any indication, the next few days would be blissful.

When she finally made her way up the sand, an older guy approached, looking remarkably fit for someone with a head full of white hair.

"Excuse me, would you and your husband be interested in playing a game of volleyball with us? Our friends couldn't make it, but we really want to play and have six people so far. We'd love to make it eight so there'd be four on each side."

Husband?

Naphressa opened her mouth to correct his mistake, but didn't. She didn't mind at all that he thought she was married to Axel.

"Let me check with Axel and find out. My name is Naphressa." She extended her hand and he shook it.

"Roger. If Axel says yes, we're right over there." He pointed down the beach, and a group of people with a volleyball waved at them.

She waved back. "If it's a go, I'll give you the thumbs-up, and we'll meet you over there."

Roger walked away and she ran up the beach to where Axel was reclining under the umbrella with dark shades on.

"What was that about?" he asked.

"We got invited to participate in a volleyball game. Are you up for it?" She didn't doubt he would be. In the short time she'd come to know him, she knew Axel was very competitive.

He sat up. "I haven't played volleyball in a long time. I'm not even sure I remember the rules, but I'm up for a game."

"Perfect. Oh, by the way, they think we're married." She looked down the beach and gave Roger the thumbs-up. He waved his acknowledgement.

She turned her attention back to Axel, who was looking at her.

"You want to correct them, about us being married?"

Naphressa shrugged dismissively. "I don't care if you don't."

"I definitely don't care." He stood and held out a hand to her. "Come along, wife. Let's go kick some butt."

She placed her hand in his, thinking about what it would be like to be his wife for real, not pretend. To wake up every morning next to his firm body. To be hugged and kissed and cherished, and to have his warm sense of humor cheering her up whenever she was in a bad mood. With Axel, joy was a constant companion, and smiles became her favorite facial expression.

Being married to him would be like heaven, and all of a sudden, she wanted that very much. More than anything, she wanted that life, in that four-bedroom house with a basement and the fish. She wanted full breakfasts, hot sex instead of breakfast, and wrestling with the kids. She wanted it all, and she wanted it with him.

They met with the volleyball participants, introductions were made, and the game began. Two women and two men on each side. They ended up on Roger's team with his wife.

Axel was competitive, but the people they were playing with were highly competitive, too. Back and forth they went, jumping high, spiking the ball over the net. A few times Naphressa dived to keep the ball from hitting the sand, but failed in her attempt, instead sputtering in annoyance when sand dusted up into her face. The teams were pretty evenly matched, but when all was said and done, they pulled out a win by two points.

"Great game," Roger said, as they high-fived each other.

"Do the two of you have dinner plans?" Roger's wife asked. She had graying hair and wasn't as fit as Roger but had the energy of a much younger woman. "You're welcome to join us after we leave and get cleaned up."

"You should come. That'll give us a chance to rub their noses in the loss even more," Roger said.

"We can hear you," a woman from the opposing team yelled.

The four of them laughed.

Naphressa glanced at Axel. "You want to?"

"Let's do it."

"Great!" Roger gave them his number and Axel gave them his.

They then parted ways and Axel and Naphressa headed back up the beach to their spot in the sand.

"That was fun," she said, taking a swig of the water that she'd pulled from the cooler.

"It was," Axel agreed. He tipped his head back and drained his bottle.

"This weekend was exactly what I needed," Naphressa said quietly.

His gaze caressed her face. "Me, too."

16

D inner with Roger and his friends ended up lasting late into the night over drinks and lots of laughs. Before separating, they promised to keep in touch. By the time Naphressa and Axel returned to the condo, Naphressa was exhausted from the long day and barely managed to undress before falling into bed. Axel joined her soon after and they slept soundly through the night.

The next morning they ate breakfast on the balcony, which Naphressa cooked this time, while Axel mapped out their sightseeing plans. After the meal, they left for the Gullah Heritage Trail Tour, led by the people of Gullah descent—descendants of enslaved Africans who cultivated and harvested the Sea Islands cotton and had managed to preserve much of the linguistic and cultural aspects of their African ancestors.

During the two-hour tour, Naphressa and Axel learned about their food, language, and traditions, as well as explored a Gullah family compound. Later, they ate lunch at a restaurant that offered traditional lowcountry cuisine, and then set off to visit several museums and the red and white lighthouse in

Harbor Town. They arrived back at the condo near the end of the day.

"I need a shower, to freshen up before dinner," Naphressa said. Being out all day, she'd gotten sweaty and because they'd had to rush to dinner with Roger and the others last night, she'd only rinsed her hair instead of washing it. Tonight she wanted to do a thorough shampoo and condition.

"You go first. I need to call my dad. No telling how long that conversation will last," Axel said, looking down at his phone. His father had texted while they were at the lighthouse.

"I'm going to be in there for a while," she said.

"That's fine." He looked up at her. "If you take too long, I'll come get you out."

"Ha. Not if I can help it."

Naphressa left him in the living room and in the master bedroom stripped out of her shorts and top. She went into the adjourning bathroom and opened the frameless glass door to the large shower filled with aquamarine and sand-colored tumbled tile. Turning on the water, she lifted her face to the lukewarm spray and stood there for a few minutes letting the water saturate her thick hair and slough off the dirt and grime of the day.

She picked up the shampoo bottle and suddenly realized she wasn't alone. Axel watched her from across the room, one shoulder resting on the frame of the door.

"Finished with your conversation?"

"Yeah. He didn't want much. He needed to confirm that everything was fine with the condo. Then I thought I'd come in here to see if you needed any help."

"Is that right?"

"Mhmm. So do you? Need help?"

"As a matter of fact, I do."

Axel grabbed the back of his T-shirt and pulled it over his head. His jeans and socks followed swiftly to the floor. Confident in his nakedness, he walked across the tile and stepped into the shower.

Without a word, he took the shampoo, and Naphressa faced the wall. Axel squirted the creamy product into his hands and rubbed it into her hair. A nice lather formed and Naphressa smelled the tropical fragrance from the essential oils. She had never had a man wash her hair before and wanted to enjoy every minute of the experience. Closing her eyes, she succumbed to the wholly sensual act of his blunt fingertips massaging her scalp.

"How does that feel?" Axel asked.

"Good. So darn good."

He chuckled softly, the throaty, masculine sound stoking the fire that had been slowly brought to life within her.

Axel rinsed her hair. After a second shampoo and rinse, he added conditioner. Carefully smoothing the viscous liquid throughout, he took his time to ensure each strand was fully coated.

Eyes still closed, Naphressa moaned softly.

"Careful now," he said.

"You're doing such a good job," she said. "If the lawyer thing doesn't work out, you could always get a job as a shampoo boy."

"It's important to always have a plan B," he quipped.

After he rinsed the conditioner from her hair, Naphressa soaped a washcloth and faced him.

"Now it's my turn to take care of you."

"Oh yeah?" His eyes lit up.

"Mhmm." She rubbed the soapy rag over his neck and chest. She was thorough in the washing, taking care to get his back, ass, thick thighs, and feet. Back in the front, his erection jutted at her, proud and tempting—and she couldn't resist the temptation. She cleaned his genitals and took pleasure in how his heavy-lidded eyes observed her actions, his stomach tight as he held his breath under her ministrations.

Reveling in her power, Naphressa stroked his tumescent length, alternating between hard and gentle caresses, laughing softly when he whispered a series of curses. She lowered before him and, emboldened by his sharp inhale, took the tip in her mouth and went to work. When she sucked him deeper, mouth stretched around the circumference of his erection, Axel fell back against the tile with a groan, biting his bottom lip and lifting his head toward the ceiling.

Using the weapons at her disposal—her hands and mouth—Naphressa kept him pinned to the wall so he could receive all the pleasure she wanted to give.

One hand fastened into her wet hair. "Baby, baby," he whispered, sounding breathless. Water ran down his dark skin in rivulets, and again she was mesmerized by his godlike appearance.

She continued to work her mouth like a suction, and knowing he was close only increased her excitement. Making soft moaning noises so he knew how much she enjoyed the act, she moved her hands over his pelvis and thighs, massaging and bringing him closer to orgasm.

"I'm coming."

That was her only warning before his knees dipped. With a loud grunt, he quickly straightened against the wall, grabbed the back of her head, and ejaculated into her mouth. When he'd expelled every drop, he shuddered and released her.

Satisfied with her performance, Naphressa stood and soaped her skin while a depleted Axel looked on, his body limp against the tile.

"You're something else, you know that?" he said.

She tossed a saucy grin over her shoulder at him. "Thank you."

As she rinsed the soap from her skin, his arms came around her waist. "No woman has ever made me need her as much as you have." His hands smoothed over the roundness of her hips and his lips teased the skin on the side of her neck. "I want to be inside you."

"Now?"

"Now."

He reached in front of her and turned off the water. They towel-dried their bodies and her hair, but her raven tresses remained damp.

In the bedroom, she said, "My hair's still wet. We'll mess up the bed."

"I don't give a damn," Axel said in a determined voice.

They lowered onto the bed and made love like it was the first time, their kisses slow and intense as they explored each other with leisurely licks and touches. She caressed him everywhere, her fingers laying claim to his broad shoulders and playing with the hairs on his chest. Under her palms, his warm skin had been cooled by the water and with a swipe of her tongue, tasted clean.

Nothing and no one had ever made her feel as good as this man did, and she ached to be one with him, her hips tilting upward to demand he join their bodies sooner rather than later.

Finally, he grasped her knees and eased her legs wider. He slid home while maintaining eye contact, and she felt their connection deep in her chest, the same as she'd experienced during their short time together in Belize. Axel had all the traits any woman would want in a husband. A sense of humor, a gentle and caring attitude, and love-making skills that made her want to jump his bones on a regular basis.

He filled her all the way to the hilt and pushed his hips back and forth in slow motion. She gasped from the torturous movement, fingernails sinking into his side as she was tossed on a sea of pleasure, delirious with passion.

A slow-rolling orgasm took charge of her body and curled her toes, back arching as she let out a series of whimpers and grabbed his tight butt. Their rhythm matched as they rode out the storm together, the only sounds the creaking of the bed and their harsh breaths.

Afterward, Naphressa lay curled against his side, heart racing, and admitted to herself that she loved Axel Becker —*needed* him—and wanted him in her life for good.

17

Axel woke her up by lying on her back, but his weight was not too heavy because he supported himself on his elbows.

"Get up, sleepyhead. It's late, and we need to decide about dinner."

Naphressa had dozed after sex. She squinted at the lamp that was turned on next to the bed. Outside was dark, and the clock beside the bed said it was after nine.

"I have something you can eat," Naphressa said with a naughty smile.

"Guess what? I got something for you, too." Axel pumped his hips, his semi-hard penis bumping repeatedly against the crease of her bottom through the sheet.

Naphressa cracked up. "Please get that thing away from me."

"You weren't saying that a couple of hours ago."

He continued to hump her, and in typical fashion, her desire ignited and she wanted more of him. He was like a drug that her body constantly craved. She needed him daily but would take him hourly if she could.

Two could play his little game. Naphressa spread her legs so he fell between them and gyrated her hips in a sexy, circular motion.

Axel swore. "You're not playing fair," he muttered.

He dragged the sheet lower and rained kisses down her bare back. Moving lower until his lips touched her bottom, his actions built an almost unbearable tension between her wide open legs.

"Axel, what are you doing?" she asked in a pained voice, knowing exactly what he was about to do. What she wanted him to do. What he loved to do.

"Getting something to eat," he answered in a whisper.

His tongue flicked across the lower edge of her left ass cheek and then went deeper, seeking out her clit. When the tip touched the tight bundle of nerves, she let out a gasp. Her fingers curled into the soft pillows as he lifted her hips from the bed and devoured her from behind, pressing his face deep between her legs. He gorged on her wet flesh, merciless in his determination to satisfy. Holding her thighs wide, his tongue plundered her folds while his lips plucked constantly at her swollen clit. Every lick and suck was magnified by the way he held her thighs apart, and the groans of pleasure he made only added to the sensuality of the act.

Right before she came, her body tightened, becoming as rigid and stiff as a baton. A scream got trapped in her throat, and she took her own breasts in hand and squeezed the taut nipples. The pillow stifled her screams when she came, eyes squeezed tight, trembling until she descended from her high—sated, relaxed.

Axel left the room, probably to clean his face. When he returned, he flopped onto his back on the pillow next to her.

Weak, Naphressa remained prone on the mattress and opened one eye. "Give me a minute, and I'll hook you up, too."

He chuckled. "I'm good, sweetheart. You took real good care of me in the shower."

"I want to."

"I'm good."

He turned on his side. Her chest tightened at the look of adoration in his eyes. He meant it. He didn't need her to reciprocate right then, which made her want to take him into her mouth even more, to once again give him pleasure the same way he'd given her.

"I want to ask you something that I've wondered about for a while. I didn't bring up the topic sooner because I knew it would be touchy, but I feel like we've come a long way in our relationship, and I can ask you this now. Why did you continue wearing your wedding ring after your husband died?"

"Lots of widows and widowers continue to wear their rings long after the death of their spouses. Some never take them off."

"But why did *you* continue to wear yours? And for so long afterward. My initial thought was that you might still be in love with your dead husband, but after all you've told me, I know that's not the case."

"I'm definitely no longer in love with him." Naphressa's voice was emphatic. She didn't want there to be any misunderstanding between them. She pulled the sheet over her naked body and repositioned so that she faced Axel. "There were so many reasons why I couldn't remove the ring right away. At first I kept it on, thinking I'd remove it after the funeral. We'd been married for five years, so what was another week or two? It didn't feel right to remove it before that time.

"Then we heard he'd receive a posthumous hero's award for his bravery, and I couldn't take it off until after that ceremony— at least *I* thought so. For weeks after the ceremony, people expressed their sorrow and admiration of his heroism and made comments about his bravery and the sacrifice he made.

That made finding the right time to take off the ring harder. Right when I thought the appropriate amount of time had passed, I ran into Kathy Hayes in the hall. We spoke briefly. I can't remember the details, but it was work-related, for sure. Near the end of the conversation, she took my left hand in hers, and tears filled her eyes. 'You miss him, too,' she said. I couldn't tell her that I didn't, and I felt like crap. I didn't want Byron to die, but I didn't miss him because I'd stopped loving him. Our marriage was in name only when he passed. So, it seemed I had missed my window to take off the ring.

"I decided to keep it on a little bit longer, and the weeks stretched into months. On more than one occasion, I've noted Victor looking at my hand, and it became clear that he *expected* me to continue wearing the ring—without saying a word. I knew if I took it off, I would be gone. Selfish, I know."

There was no judgment in Axel's eyes. "It's called survival. You did what you had to do," he said.

Naphressa traced circles in the white sheet with her fingernail. "You know I take it off at night, when I remove all my other jewelry, and I thought if I could prove my worth to the company over time, I'd eventually be able to remove the ring permanently and no one would bat an eye. Now I realize how flawed my thought process was. I backed myself into a corner because of my own insecurities."

"Tough lesson to learn," Axel remarked.

"Tell me about it." She moved closer to him and placed her head on his pillow. "I'm definitely leaving Hayes Realty after the Brixton deal is signed. I know I've told you before, but I mean it. I'll get my bonus and then turn in my resignation. After I paid off some personal debts, I saved quite a bit of money during the four years Byron and I were together because I didn't have to spend much. I should be fine if I can find another job in about six months or so."

"He was a rich man. Did he leave you anything?"

"He didn't have anything to leave me. People thought he was a millionaire, but the truth is, the house we lived in belonged to his parents. I moved out not long after he passed and rented my townhouse. There were a few thousand dollars in our mutual account, but that's it. Byron earned a salary at the company, enough for the average person to live comfortably, but not enough to afford the lavish lifestyle he indulged in. The cars, the expensive vacations, the jewelry and other gifts he gave his mistresses—all of that was subsidized by his parents. That's why he appeased them by marrying me."

"To keep the flow of money coming."

"Yes. Plus getting married demonstrated he was mature and responsible, which was important for them to see since he was the sole heir."

"When you walk away from Hayes Realty, whatever happens, you know I got you. Anything you need, I'm there," Axel said.

"I know."

"Do you? Do you really understand what I'm saying?" His left hand cupped her nape, warm and comforting.

"I do, and I appreciate it."

His eyes became very intense as they looked into hers. "I'm trying to tell you what you mean to me, Naphressa. I'd do anything for you. I love you."

The air stilled, and her heart began a riotous beating in her chest. Tears misted her eyes, but she had no idea why she was about to cry except that his words were her extremely emotional.

"Axel, do you mean it?" she whispered. "You love me?"

"I wouldn't say it if I didn't. I don't use those words lightly. You're sexy and funny and smart as hell. When a man knows, he knows, baby. You're it for me. I love you."

Naphressa flung herself on top of him and kissed his lips like she was starving and he was her last chance at sustenance.

She caressed his bearded cheek and looked down into his eyes. "I love you, too," she whispered against his lips. He'd allayed her fears and made her believe in love again.

How could she have made the mistake of thinking he was like Byron? Her husband had been outwardly kind and unassuming, but behind closed doors he was unkind and selfish. Axel, on the other hand, was the real deal. Outwardly arrogant, some might say cocky, he was actually quite tender and his protectiveness made her feel as if she had a dependable teammate—someone to help her win in the game of life.

A sexy grin spread across his face. His dark eyes brightened with the same happiness that must be reflected in her own, to know that after years of misery and choosing wrong the first time, there was no doubt they had chosen correctly this time.

She gazed down into his handsome face. "All I ever wanted was for Byron to love me," she said. "But he didn't. I wish you and I had met before. My life would be so different."

"Let's not worry about the past. Byron is gone, and Rose is gone, but we're together now. I promise to give you all the love you need and deserve."

18

The halls were mostly empty as Naphressa walked to the copy room with the phone to her ear. She was high off the long weekend she'd spent with Axel. Despite all the fun activities, the highlight had been when they declared their love for each other. How lucky was she to have found a man like him? Someone needed to pinch her!

"I hate you have to work late tonight," she said into the phone.

"This brief won't write itself," Axel replied, regret heavy in his tone.

Naphressa stopped before the copy machine and slipped the two pages into the feeder. "When will I see you again?" she asked, lowering her voice.

"Not until Friday. I'll be working long hours the next few days."

"You can't sneak in a little time for me tomorrow?" Who was she? First she'd limited them to Fridays only, but now here she was on a Tuesday afternoon fiending for Axel. And they'd recently spent four glorious and fun-filled days together!

"Afraid so."

She glanced over her shoulder to make sure that she was alone. "I should come by your office and get a quickie. Something to hold me over until Friday."

"Oh yeah?" Axel said, voice lowered.

"Well, we christened my office, so it's only fair that we christen yours, too."

He groaned. "Baby, don't torture me like this."

Naphressa spoke in her sultriest voice. "Say the word, and I'll be there to give you a break, by mouth or hand, or any way you like."

Axel swore softly. "I can't see you tonight for sure. Our whole team is working late, and we're having dinner brought in. You have plans tomorrow night?

"I have absolutely no plans. Unless something changes, I'll be sitting at home, twiddling my thumbs since I can't spend the night with you."

Seeing him and talking to him had become a necessary part of her life. She didn't know how she wound up in this position, but she didn't want to leave it. Being with him felt so good, so right. Had she known that this was what a real relationship should feel like, she would never have accepted Byron's marriage proposal.

"In that case, we're getting together tomorrow night. I'll call about an hour or so before I plan to leave work and then you can come to the house. Does that sound good?"

"Yes. I'll see you tomorrow. Love you."

"Love you, too, baby."

Naphressa blew him a kiss through the phone and hung up.

"Who was that?"

She swung around and to her horror saw Victor standing behind her. Her heart darn near leaped into her throat. "Victor."

"Who was that?" he asked again, in a steelier tone of voice.

"A friend."

"A friend. That phone call sounded like more than a friend to me."

She wanted to ask how much of the conversation he'd overhead but was afraid to hear the answer.

"My son has barely been dead a year, and you're already sleeping around?" Anger flickered across his face.

"I am *not* sleeping around."

"No? Then tell me who that was."

Naphressa straightened her spine. Mentally, she was in a much better place than months ago and would not let him bully her. "I don't think that's any of your business," she said, in a firm tone.

"Is that right?"

Fear trickled down her spine. She didn't like the expression in his eyes, the way they'd narrowed and turned hard.

"It was a personal conversation."

"While on company time. You may not like to hear this, but while you're here, we expect you to do your work. Anything less is unprofessional."

"I do my work, and I'm always professional." That was one thing she would not let anyone accuse her of being—unprofessional.

"We have a problem, Naphressa."

"And what would that be?"

"I don't think that we can trust you anymore." His head lifted to a haughtier angle than normal.

"Where is this coming from? I was having a private conversation with someone—"

"Someone who you refuse to give any details about and refuse to tell me the nature of your relationship with. But I don't need you to tell me because I'm well aware of what's going on. Quite frankly, I find it disturbing that you've moved on already. Makes me wonder if wearing Byron's ring means anything to you at all." His scathing gaze lanced down at her left hand and the ring she wore. "Is it all for show? Did you even love my son?"

"Of course I loved him." Once upon a time, before they grew apart and she learned about his affairs. "But Byron is dead, and you can't expect me to be alone forever, Victor."

"Not forever, but surely you can forego screwing around and tarnishing our good name."

"Oh for goodness sake, I am not tarnishing your name. If anyone tarnished the Hayes name—" She ended the sentence abruptly.

"What were you about to say?" Victor asked, low and slow.

Heart racing, Naphressa made a decision to say what she should have said long ago. It was time Victor knew the truth about his son. "I went through a lot with Byron."

"Don't you dare speak ill of my dead son. He was a hero!" Victor snapped.

"Yes, he was a hero, but he was a terrible husband. He was cheating on me. He was a womanizer. I found out he'd cheated on me the entire time we were together with numerous women."

"I don't believe you. Stop it!" Victor barked.

"It's true!"

"You're a liar, simply trying to tarnish his good name to save your own dirty reputation," he seethed.

"The last year of our marriage was all pretend. Once I confronted him about the cheating, he didn't hide his affairs anymore. I don't know how many women there were, but there were multiple."

"And why did you stay? I'll tell you why, because you got something out of the marriage, didn't you? You were quite the social climber. We allowed you into *our* world. You seduced him, convinced him to marry you, and then used your position as his wife and a member of the family to work your way into the position you have now. Project manager—we gave you the position of project manager—despite you not having a college education or any prior experience or certifications in that area."

His words struck at the core of her insecurities. She could hear her father now, yelling at her mother, belittling her lack of education. She could hear Byron's words, letting her know that she had attained her role in the company because *he* had chosen her. There was nothing special about her.

Naphressa refused to doubt herself any longer and fisted one hand at her side. "My work ethic got me to where I am."

"I'm not so sure about that. Perhaps we need to reevaluate your role at Hayes Realty."

He was about to do what she'd feared all along. "Victor, don't be rash."

"We need to have a meeting with Kathy to discuss these latest developments. Byron is no longer here, and I'm not convinced we really need you anymore."

"I'm working on the Brixton project, and it's not complete. I'm a good manager, and you know it." She hated that her voice trembled at the end.

"As I said, perhaps we need to do an evaluation. Come with me, please." He stalked away, clearly expecting her to follow.

Naphressa left the two sheets in the feeder and followed more slowly, dread pounding away in her stomach. This was actually what she had been afraid of all along—the possibility of losing her job because Byron's parents no longer wanted her there, and he more or less said that.

She sat on the edge of the ornate couch in the outer office in Victor's suite of offices. She clutched her phone, wondering if she should make a quick call to her sister or Axel, but she was too afraid to move, much less dial either of their numbers.

Victor's assistant had only asked her if she wanted something to drink, and after that she had turned her attention to her computer. Naphressa listened to her fingers move rapidly across the keyboard, the constant tapping loud and annoying in the quiet of the room.

The meeting between Victor and Kathy lasted about fifteen minutes before he called her into his office. She stood slowly and walked in to hear the verdict. Victor stood with his arms crossed in front of the desk. Kathy, looking poised and emotionless in a burgundy suit, stood next to him with a string of pearls around her neck and her chestnut skin covered in pancakelike layers of makeup.

"Kathy and I talked, and we've made a decision. In truth, we should've made this decision a long time ago. After Byron passed, we didn't want to toss you out on the street. You were, after all, his wife. But it seems you've moved on, and perhaps it's time for us to move on, as well."

"You can't be serious."

Naphressa had suspected this would be the outcome if they found out she was seeing another man, but having her dismissal actually play out still took her by surprise. Could they really be this petty and vindictive?

The door behind her opened, and Randy, the guard from downstairs, entered.

"You can remove her from the premises," Victor said calmly.

Naphressa's mouth fell open. "Victor, Kathy, is this really necessary?'

Victor's expression was icy cold. "Remove her from the premises. *Now*," he said to Randy.

With an apologetic expression, Randy approached.

She sidestepped him. "You don't have to touch me. Can I at least get my personal things from the office?" she asked Victor.

The older man nodded, and without another word, Naphressa left the office on barely functioning legs. She didn't know how they didn't fold under her as she stopped to pick up an empty box in the copy room. She then proceeded to her office, averting her eyes and flinching internally at the curious stares from employees on the way there. Randy stood guard outside the open door until she'd gathered her paintings, purse, and other knickknacks. She hoped she hadn't forgotten anything, but she'd reach out to Loretta later. She could count on her making sure she received any items of value left behind.

Naphressa handed Randy her building pass without a word, and he followed her as she walked back out toward the front. Loretta was coming in from lunch and stopped short. Her gaze quickly swept over Randy, Naphressa, and the box.

"Naphressa, darlin', what's going on?" she asked, though it was clear from her horrified expression that she knew exactly what was going on.

Naphressa gulped back the humiliation. "Today is my last day. Goodbye, Loretta."

"I don't—I don't understand..."

"It's been a pleasure working with you." Balancing the box on her right hip, she pulled Loretta into a one-armed hug, but the woman was so stunned by the unfolding events she didn't hug her back.

"Naphressa, honey, please, talk to me."

Naphressa shook her head and blinked back tears. "I'll call you later. Goodbye," she whispered.

She continued her walk of shame out the door with Randy close behind her. They rode the elevator to the first floor in silence, and he made sure to walk her out the glass doors at the front.

"Goodbye, Naphressa. I'm really sorry about this." He grimaced and cast his eyes toward the ground.

"It's okay, Randy. I know you were just doing your job. Goodbye."

Head held high, she walked to her car and dropped the box in the back seat.

The tears didn't fall until she was halfway home.

19

Axel leaned on the doorbell outside Naphressa's townhouse.

He'd been calling her since yesterday, and other than a short text saying she didn't feel well and wanted to be alone, she hadn't responded again.

It was now Thursday afternoon, and with work out of the way, he'd reached out, only to have his message ignored. Well, she couldn't avoid him forever.

"Naphressa, open the door! Open it now, or I'll have to assume something is wrong with you, and I'll break it down."

He waited, anxiously flexing the fingers of his left hand, fully prepared to back up and deliver a running kick that would knock the door out its frame. Luckily, nothing so dramatic was necessary. Naphressa came to the door looking like...crap.

Her eyes were red and puffy, and her hair pulled back into a messy ponytail that did more to highlight its uncombed condition than convey any semblance of order. She wore a green and white terry-cloth robe over what appeared to be a white T-shirt with a yellow—mustard?—stain near the collar.

"What happened? What's wrong?" Axel rushed forward and pulled her into his arms.

She collapsed against him and started crying into his neck, her quiet sobs slowly stripping away the outer layers of his heart. Her pain became his pain, and he was determined to bring back order and peace to her life. He backed them away from the door so he could close it, and with one arm around her shoulders led Naphressa to the sofa in the living room and sat beside her.

Taking her shoulders, he looked at her, remaining calm though he wanted to rip apart whoever or whatever was causing her pain. "Sweetheart, talk to me. What happened?"

"They..." She sniffed. "They fired me, Axel. Victor Hayes overheard me talking to you on Tuesday, and he immediately fired me."

Another bout of crying started, and he pulled her into his arms again, rubbing her back and allowing her time to let out all the emotion. He couldn't believe this had happened on Tuesday and he'd only now found out. He would have come sooner—in the middle of the night—if he'd had any indication she was suffering.

When she finally calmed down, he went into the kitchen and brought back a bottle of water. She gratefully drank half before setting it on the table in front of them.

"Explain to me exactly what happened."

"I tried to talk to him and explain it was unfair to expect me to remain loyal to Byron, but that didn't work." Her voice trembled on every word. "Then I told him about Byron's infidelities, but he called me a liar and said I was tarnishing his good name to save my reputation." She laughed bitterly. "The funny thing is, I think he knew."

"About Byron's cheating?"

Naphressa nodded. "Something about the way he responded—surprised, but not really surprised. Upset, but not really upset. He *knew* Byron had stepped out on me but was determined to pretend otherwise and protect the reputation of the hero, his beloved only child. Anyway, he said he needed to consult with Kathy, but that was a delay tactic. Everybody knows Victor makes all the major decisions in the company and doesn't need Kathy's permission for anything. Thirty minutes later I was being escorted from the premises by security. It was humiliating." She picked at her fingernails.

Axel took her hands in his. "Sweetheart, I'm sorry you went through that. What can I do? How can I help?"

"There's nothing you can do. I have to accept that I've lost my job and move on."

"What about the Brixton project? Who's going to finish that?

"Probably Victor. I can't see him passing it on to someone else because it's too important. It's the biggest and most important project the company has ever undertaken."

"All the more reason why you should be involved. You helped them get this project, and to cut you out isn't right."

She gave him a watery smile. "He has every right to fire me if he wants to, and there's nothing I can do about it. Besides, I don't know that I *want* to do anything about it. The most important part is that the buyout goes through and the employees' jobs are saved."

They both fell silent while the wheels turned in Axel's brain. "That's not good enough for me," he said grimly.

Naphressa looked at him. "What do you mean? This has nothing to do with you."

"Losing your job has everything to do with me, and I'm not going to sit here and do nothing while you suffer."

Her fingers tightened on his. "Whatever you have planned, get it out of your mind. I don't need you to do anything."

"Can't do that. You told me before that you suspected you would lose your job if Victor and Kathy found out that you were with someone. They did, and you lost your job. What do you think is going to happen next? How did Byron threaten you, very specifically? Your livelihood."

She thought for a minute, and then her eyes widened. "They're going to blackball me."

Axel nodded. "Exactly. But we're not going to let them get away with this."

"But what can you do? What can I do?" Her voice was shaking again, and he squeezed her hands to reassure her. "Let me handle it. I need a bit of time to think, but I'm sure that I can come up with a solution."

"Your firm represents them in this transaction. Wouldn't it be a conflict for you to get involved?"

"There are ways around every potential obstacle. Like I said, let me handle it. In the meantime, when was the last time you've eaten?"

Her shoulders slumped. "I barely remember. The past couple of days have been a blur. This morning, sometime, I think. I ate a bag of corn chips. I haven't wanted to eat or do much, to be honest."

"Here's what we're going to do. You're going to go upstairs and take a shower and comb your hair."

Her face softened. "I look like crap, don't I?"

"Yeah, you kinda do." He smiled and dropped a kiss to her forehead. "While you're getting ready, I'll make reservations for dinner. I'm taking you out of here, putting some food in your belly, and making sure that you take care of yourself for the rest of the day, okay?"

"Okay," she said reluctantly.

"You can't let them get you down. You've worked too hard to get to where you are, and you deserve every accolade and to celebrate every accomplishment. You've earned them through hard work, not by the way they want to make you think you earned it—only because you were their daughter-in-law.

They're about to have some serious growth because of *your* hard work. Don't let anyone tell you otherwise."

She gulped and nodded. Her shoulders straightened and she lifted her head higher. "You're right."

"That's my baby. Now, go upstairs, and let me make some calls."

She rose from the sofa. She took two steps and then turned around and looked at him. "I'm so glad you're here. Thank you."

He smiled, and she disappeared down the hall.

Axel pulled out his phone and dialed the number of a friend who worked in employment law at another law firm. Victor and Kathy Hayes thought they could mess with his woman? Hell, no. He was about to handle their asses real quick.

When his friend answered, he said, "Hey, Jocelyn, I need your help with something..."

20

A xel rang Naphressa's bell and waited for her to come to the door. After a few seconds, she arrived, greeting him with a wide smile and looking much more relaxed and happier than when he'd seen her on Thursday.

After dinner, they'd spent the evening together. The next day, he arranged for a car to pick her up and take her to a spa, where she had an entire day of pampering while he worked. When he picked her up for their Friday night date, she was in much better spirits.

He left her early Saturday morning so he and Jocelyn could hash out a contract that he believed would be beneficial to Naphressa. No way was he letting those people railroad her out of a job she loved with nothing to show for it. Especially since she'd placed the greatest deal in the history of their company right into their laps.

"Hey," Naphressa said.

She gave him a hug, and he pulled her soft body into his, taking a moment to inhale her unique scent into his nostrils. It was getting harder and harder to be away from her. The days seemed never-ending, and the nights torturous. At some point they needed to have a serious conversation about the direction their relationship was going in.

"I have something for you." Axel held up the envelope that contained the contract he and Jocelyn had written.

"Okay," Naphressa said, sounding cautious.

He followed her into the living room and sat down beside her on the sofa.

"Like I told you, Jocelyn is one of the best. She discussed all the possibilities with me. At the end of the day, you're right, they can fire you if they want to, but that didn't sit well with me, because you haven't done anything wrong. The only reason they're firing you is because they wanted to keep you under their thumb a little bit longer. Maybe brag to their friends about how loyal their son's widow was to them. So, I talked to her about some possibilities, including the fact that you're the reason why they have the Brixton deal. She suggested you go back to them and demand a payout based on your work contribution."

"They'll never agree to that," she said, flipping through the pages.

"You might be right, but would they be willing to fight you in court?"

She lifted her gaze.

"Jocelyn and I discussed multiple scenarios, including that they would want you to keep quiet about their son's infidelities, and the fact that they cut you out of such a huge deal. All of that is written into this confidential contract that will remain sealed. You stay quiet and they stay quiet. If they breach their side of the deal, you go to court and get paid."

"How much?"

"Take a look at the middle of page four, under *Compensation*."

She flipped to the appropriate page and her eyes popped open wider. "Five million dollars?"

"You're in a great position. Their emotional, over-the-top reaction to you finding someone else and possibly exposing their son for the not-so-perfect person he really was, tells me everything I need to know."

"You're so confident."

She deserved nothing but the best, and he'd make sure she got it. "Because I'm right. If you want to get what you deserve financially, and you want to keep your reputation in Atlanta's commercial real estate industry, then you have to give as good as you get. And this is the way to do it. Take a look at the terms."

He flipped the pages for her and tapped the section he wanted her to pay attention to. "If they agree—which I have no doubt they will—all of The Brixton Group employees will get a position in the newly formed company, like you asked. You'll walk away with over a million dollars like you told me you wanted, a glowing letter of recommendation, and your reputation intact. We hear a peep of negativity surrounding your decision to leave—*your* decision, not theirs—and we go after them in court, guns blazing—at the end of which, you walk away with five million dollars. Frankly, based on my experience, I'm certain Victor has way more to hide than his son's extramarital affairs. People in his position always do, and there's no telling what we'll find once discovery starts."

Naphressa's brow wrinkled and she sat for a moment in silence. He waited patiently while she mulled everything he'd said.

Finally, she inhaled and let out a deep breath. "You've convinced me. Let's do it. I only wish I could see their faces when they get this."

"If I could, I'd hand deliver it myself and sit while they read every word," Axel joked.

"You're enjoying this way too much," Naphressa said, amused.

"Maybe a little bit. I have to be honest, I always thought you were worried about nothing. No way they'd let you go because you'd found a new man. But I was wrong. I also feel partially responsible because I was on the other end of the line when Victor overheard our conversation."

"It's no one's fault. Like you said all along, it was ridiculous. They acted like...like they owned me." She shivered.

Axel rubbed a soothing hand up and down her arm.

Naphressa smiled at him. "You kick ass, you know that? I like that my man's a lawyer." She climbed onto his lap and looped her arms around his neck. He readjusted his position so that she was lined up right over his pelvis.

"And you put in all this work in such a short amount of time, for little ole me. I must have really put it on you," she said.

Smoothing his hands down her back, Axel brought them to rest on the rise of her bottom. "It's not about sex. You mean everything to me, and seeing you hurt pissed me off. I'm not letting anyone get away with hurting the woman I love. There will always be repercussions for that."

Her eyes softened. "I'm so glad we met. I love you so much."

"Love you, too, baby."

Their kiss was soft and wet and intimate.

"Mmm. Angry Axel is such a turn on," Naphressa whispered against his mouth.

"Oh yeah? Let me get angry more often, then."

She laughed, nuzzling his neck.

"There's something I've been meaning to do for a while." Axel fished in his pocket and held up two keys on a keychain.

"What's this?"

"The keys to my house, so you can come and go as you please. You don't have to call first. Just come over and come in. I'll also get you a remote for the garage."

"That's a big step."

"Pretty huge, but we're ready, don't you think?"

She grinned broadly. "Yes, we are."

EPILOGUE

Naphressa used her key and pushed through the front door of Axel's house, barely able to contain her excitement.

"I got the job!" she hollered.

Last year, she took advantage of the million-dollar hush money she'd received from Victor and Kathy Hayes and took a month-long break before she started job-hunting. There weren't a lot of available positions in her field, and fewer that interested her or offered the salary she wanted.

About six months ago, she heard rumors about a soon-to-be-available lead project manager opening. After some research into the position and the company culture, she decided this was the job she wanted and applied when they started taking applications. When they stopped advertising for the position, she was one of five candidates they called for an interview. After two intense interviews and a personality assessment that lasted half a day, Naphressa was now the lead project manager for R&J Construction Company.

"Axel?" She followed the scent of simmering spaghetti sauce into the kitchen, but he wasn't there.

What she did find made her pull up short. Julienned basil leaves sat on the chopping board, and right next to them on the counter was a Tiffany-blue box, open to reveal a beautiful emerald-cut diamond ring.

Axel came in through the door leading from the deck with a handful of more basil leaves and froze.

"What's this?" Naphressa asked quietly.

"Dammit, Naphressa, you weren't supposed to see that yet! It was supposed to be a surprise, and not tonight, either. I was planning a big proposal and..." Frustrated, Axel tossed the basil on the counter and snatched up the box. He snapped it closed.

"Yes," she whispered, answering the unasked question.

The room went silent except for the sound of the simmering sauce on the stove.

"Not like this," Axel said.

"Yes, like this. I don't need a big proposal. The answer is yes."

"No. You need a story to tell your friends and your sister and our grandkids."

"And this is the story I'll tell them. That I came by to tell you I got the job as lead project manager at R&J Construction, and I spoiled your surprise because I used the key you gave me almost a year ago. I saw the beautiful ring you'd picked out for me, and I was so overwhelmed that I said yes before you got a chance to ask me to marry you. Our story doesn't have to be perfect, Axel. It's perfect for us. I don't need the big display. I don't even want it. If you want to ask me, you can ask me, but I already gave you my answer."

"You got the job?"

"Yes."

His eyes softened. "Congratulations, baby."

"Thank you," she said, and waited impatiently for his response—for the question that came with the ring.

Eyes locked on hers, Axel came slowly forward and reopened the box. "Naphressa St. James, will you marry me?"

"Well, I'm not sure…"

"Woman, if you don't quit playing with me…" He tugged her close, and she collapsed into a fit of giggles against his chest.

"Yes, Axel Becker. My answer is yes!"

IRRESISTIBLE HUSBAND SERIES

Read the rest of the Irresistible Husband series and find out how Axel's friends, Cole and Braxton, find love!

SHOW ME by Sharon C. Cooper

Just when he thought finding a wife was out of his reach...

Colton "Cole" Eubanks is laser-focused on building wealth and settling down with a special woman before he turns forty. Accomplishing one out of two isn't bad. Unfortunately, there's no 'love of his life' on the horizon, unless he counts the one woman who's been starring in his nightly dreams—Malaya Radcliff.

After being dependent on other people for years, Malaya has finally learned to stand on her own. There's only one thing she hasn't been able to accomplish—gain full custody of her daughter. Her ex-husband never fights fair. His wealth always wins. This time Malaya's determined to come out on top. So when Cole, the man she's been secretly in lust with for over a year, makes her an offer she'd be crazy to refuse, Malaya wants to say yes. But that means sacrificing her newfound independence. Yet, his enticing proposal has her thinking—why not?

DO ME by Sheryl Lister

Staring forty in the face, Braxton Harper is accustomed to having everything in his life fall into its precise place. Only he hasn't found that special one and he refuses to settle for anything less than a woman who is his perfect match. The moment Londyn Grant dances into his life, Braxton is convinced he's found her. Kiss by sizzling kiss, the sexy doctor slowly lets her guard down. Now, if she'd only let him into her heart...

Londyn knows heartbreak. By day, the psychologist counsels others, but she has yet to find a way to heal her own heart. The last thing she wants is another relationship. However, sensual and sensitive Braxton tempts her to open up and, for the first time in her life, she's letting passion rule. But it's going to take a little therapeutic intervention—in and out of the bedroom—to get Londyn to see that this time she's found the real thing.

ALSO BY DELANEY DIAMOND

For more black romance stories, check out the Brooks Family series! In *A Passionate Love* (Brooks Family # 1), Simone Brooks meets and falls in love with nightclub owner Cameron Bennett, but will her wealth and status drive a wedge between them? Read an excerpt below.

———

She walked over to his record player against the wall and the collection of records housed in six crates around it. He could watch her walk all day and night.

"Records and a record player?" she said, quirking a brow at him.

He didn't own one of those sleek, modern ones that integrated with Bluetooth technology. His was vintage, purchased for a pittance at a garage sale.

"Don't knock it 'til you try it."

"I'm not knocking your old records, but surely you've heard of music streaming services. They're all the rage now," she quipped.

"Oh, so you got jokes."

"I'm just saying."

She shrugged with one shoulder and sent him a cute little smile before diving back into the collection. The way she angled her body over the crates made him tilt his head and imagine what he could do to her once he got her naked.

"You're a blues man. I see the old greats—B.B. King, Muddy Waters, Robert Johnson. Wow." She continued flipping. "And names I don't recognize. Do you only listen to blues?"

"Mostly blues. Some old rock, disco, etcetera. Everything's all mixed in," Cameron replied, his gaze trailing down the curve in her spine, over her bottom, and lower to her shapely calves.

"No cell phone. An old record player and records. You're an old soul, Cameron Bennett."

He lifted his gaze to hers and laughed. "You say I'm an old soul. My family says I'm stubborn."

"Well, they know you better than I do. Are you stubborn?"

"Pretty much. I like what I like, and I'm not easily distracted by every new and shiny thing."

"That's a good trait to have," she said quietly. "Mind if I put on one of the records?"

"Not at all."

She pulled one of the disks from its sleeve and placed it on the turntable. The sound of an electric guitar crackled through the old speakers as "Rock Me Baby," by B.B. King started.

"That's good music right there," Cameron said.

He left her and went into the kitchen, where steel dominated the decor. Light glinted off the steel appliances and steel built-in shelves that took the place of cabinets and exposed his collection of dishes.

He set the last of the tiramisu on a plate, added a fork, and rejoined Simone in the living room. Her eyes lit up when she saw the dessert. "Where's yours?" she asked.

Chuckling, Cameron cut a slice with the fork. "There isn't much left, so we'll have to share."

He extended the fork and she pulled the scrumptious dessert between her full lips. His stomach tightened.

"Mmm."

Cameron cut another slice and ate it. Over and over, he alternated by cutting a slice, extending it to her, and then cutting off a piece for himself to eat. All the while, King's gravelly voice serenaded them with "Rock Me Baby."

When they finished the cake, Simone brushed a crumb from the corner of her mouth and licked her lips.

He was two seconds away from ripping her clothes off. Watching her take slice after slice of cake between her red, parted lips had to be one of the most sensuous things he'd ever seen.

She kept looking at him, as if waiting for something, and that's when he realized she was waiting for him to make a move.

As the album segued into the sultrier, edgier "Blue Shadows," Cameron took Simone's hand and drew her closer, barely managing to temper the urgency beating through his blood.

"So how was it?" he asked.

"Delicious," she said softly, sounding a little breathless. "You were right, it was criminally good." She licked her lips again, and this time he knew she'd done it on purpose. "But I have a feeling that tiramisu wasn't the only reason you invited me here tonight."

One corner of Cameron's mouth ticked upward. "I have a feeling you knew that when you accepted my invitation."

His finger touched the pulse hammering at the base of her throat, and she inhaled. Her breasts lifted and stayed as she held her breath. Cameron lowered his head to the same spot and she arched her throat. When his tongue swept across the hollow between her collarbones, she released the breath as a trembling exhalation.

While B.B. King bewailed how it felt to be alone, Cameron encircled

Simone's waist with one arm and pulled her flush against his body. Cupping her face with the other hand, he went in for the kiss.

Their mouths meshed together. Slow and easy. Her lips softened beneath his, and he pried them apart to trace the edges with his tongue. She tasted sweet like the dessert they'd consumed— mascarpone cheese, amaretto, and cocoa—and his blood surged as he delved deeper into the kiss.

Simone moaned, leaning into him, and his fingers climbed into her thick hair. Angling his head, he kissed her harder, with fiercer pressure and ardent strokes of his tongue.

Drawn again to the perfumed hollow at the base of her throat, he showered kisses down the side of her neck. Her little mewl of pleasure echoed in his loins, and he pushed her against the wall, kissing her harder and more thoroughly, stroking into every corner of her mouth.

His awakening body hardened, and he lifted her high. In response, her arms immediately encircled his neck and held him tight.

Cameron turned off the phonograph and plunged the room in quiet. Moving through the house, he headed to the stairs, Simone's mouth traveling over his face and neck, her breathing irregular, her heart thudding against his chest.

Then with slow, careful steps, he started climbing up the stairs.

Get your copy of A Passionate Love now. Also available in paperback and audiobook.

ABOUT THE AUTHOR

Delaney Diamond is the USA Today Bestselling Author of sweet, sensual, passionate romance novels. Originally from the U.S. Virgin Islands, she now lives in Atlanta, Georgia. She reads romance novels, mysteries, thrillers, and a fair amount of nonfiction. When she's not busy reading or writing, she's in the kitchen trying out new recipes, dining at one of her favorite restaurants, or traveling to an interesting locale.

Enjoy free reads and the first chapter of all her novels on her website. Join her mailing list to get sneak peeks, notices of sale prices, and find out about new releases.

Join her mailing list
www.delaneydiamond.com

facebook.com/DelaneyDiamond

twitter.com/DelaneyDiamond

instagram.com/authordelaneydiamond

bookbub.com/authors/delaney-diamond

pinterest.com/delaneydiamond

Made in the USA
Columbia, SC
13 November 2020